Michael Hard
joining the Dr
was a Captain i
Director in New … Since 1963 he has been a full-time freelance author, playwright and broadcaster. Alone or with his wife Mollie he has written countless plays and dramatisations for radio, television and the stage, and over sixty books, ranging from standard literary reference works to best-selling novels. Most of the latter have been based on major films and television serials including Billy Wilder's *The Private Life of Sherlock Holmes*, Richard Lester's *The Four Musketeers* and John Houston's *The Man Who Would Be King*. The Hardwicks have been responsible for most of the *Upstairs, Downstairs* books, Michael's share, besides this volume, being *Mr Hudson's Diaries*, *Mr Bellamy's Story* and *On with the Dance*.

Also in this series and available from Sphere Books

UPSTAIRS, DOWNSTAIRS by John Hawkesworth
ROSE'S STORY by Terence Brady and Charlotte Bingham
SARAH'S STORY by Mollie Hardwick
MR HUDSON'S DIARIES by Michael Hardwick
IN MY LADY'S CHAMBER by John Hawkesworth
MR BELLAMY'S STORY by Michael Hardwick
THE YEARS OF CHANGE by Mollie Hardwick
'THE WAR TO END WARS' by Mollie Hardwick
MRS BRIDGES' STORY by Mollie Hardwick
ON WITH THE DANCE by Michael Hardwick

MRS BRIDGES' UPSTAIRS, DOWNSTAIRS COOKERY BOOK

Endings and Beginnings

MICHAEL HARDWICK

SPHERE BOOKS LIMITED
30/32 Gray's Inn Road, London WC1X 8JL

First published in Great Britain by Sphere Books Ltd 1975

Reprinted 1975, 1976

TRADE
MARK

Set in Intertype Lectura

Printed in Great Britain by
Hazell Watson & Viney Ltd,
Aylesbury, Bucks

This book is based on the latter part of the fifth television series of UPSTAIRS, DOWNSTAIRS, produced by John Hawkesworth for London Weekend Television Limited, and created by Sagitta Productions Limited in association with Jean Marsh and Eileen Atkins.

Rex Firkin was the Executive Producer, and Alfred Shaughnessy was Script Editor of the series.

The author wishes to acknowledge that in writing this book he has drawn largely on material from television scripts by the following writers:

John Hawkesworth
Jeremy Paul
Alfred Shaughnessy
Rosemary Anne Sisson

The author is grateful to them; and to London Weekend Television for the opportunity to attend recordings. He wishes to thank all connected with UPSTAIRS, DOWNSTAIRS – cast, production teams and administrators – for their co-operation and friendship.

CHAPTER ONE

'Not a penny off the pay; not a second on the day.'

It was the response of the militant new leader of the miners of South Wales to the report, published in March 1926, by Sir Herbert Samuel on the declining state of their industry. Like many official reports before and since, it proposed wide-scale reorganisation and improvements of structure, administration and working methods, but as long-term measures. The only short-term one in this case was for a cut of nearly one eighth of every miner's pay.

A. J. Cook responded characteristically. Discussion continued between the Trade Union Council and the uneasy government. A compromise seemed to be coming closer. Then, adamant in their refusal to accept wage cuts, more than a million miners were 'locked out' by the pit owners, and the incensed T.U.C. threatened a sympathy strike by more than two million workers in other industries.

The possibility of a general strike, an expedient first mooted by William Benbow in the 1820s, seemed, a century later, imminent.

'Rain and a sharp north-easterly wind, sir. Quite abnormal for the first day of May. Shall I put more coal on the fire, sir?'

Hudson hovered near the coal scuttle beside the grate in James Bellamy's sitting room. He had just drawn the curtains against the bleak dusk outside in Eaton Place.

James nodded. 'Coal fires in May! Miners out on strike and the rest of the country all jumping on the bandwagon. What a mess.'

'I gather there's still hope of a settlement, sir,' the butler said, shovelling coal. 'The Trade Union leaders are at Downing Street at this very moment, according to the wireless.'

'It shouldn't have been allowed to get this far, Hudson. A

general strike is a direct affront to the government. It should be forbidden by law.'

'I agree with you, sir. I feel ashamed of my fellow working man.'

'Not your fault, Hudson. It's men like Cook, and J. H. Thomas, and Ernest Bevin. So-called leaders with the nerve to hold the country to ransom and threaten the liberty of ordinary decent people like you.'

Hudson replaced the small shovel and straightened up.

'I understand the government have been laying in stocks of food and essential supplies for some months.'

'Oh, yes, we'll win all right. But what will it cost us? The whole world's gone stark, staring mad.'

James relapsed into dark brooding. He was only subconsciously aware of his butler's withdrawal with the announcement, 'Dinner will be at eight o'clock, sir.'

Hudson returned to the servants' hall to find his subordinates in anxious discussion.

'All army leave's been cancelled,' Edward was saying. 'There's troops roaming about all over the country.'

'Yeh, and two battleships sitting in the Mersey,' added Frederick, who had been down at the pub with Edward, listening to a Sergeant of Marines who had not needed to pay for a single drink for himself all day on the strength of his self-professed knowledge. 'They're probably going to call up the reservists.'

'Well, you're not going, Eddy,' Daisy flashed at her husband. 'You're not fighting again.'

'Who's fighting who?' asked Ruby, wide-eyed.

'Yes,' Rose challenged the handsomely impassive Frederick, 'who are you going to fight? The miners? The bus drivers?'

'Anyone who goes on strike,' he responded, unperturbed. 'Just doing our duty for the country again. Eh, Edward?'

Mr Hudson stepped in at last, as Edward opened his mouth to agree.

'That's enough of that, both of you. How many times have I told you not to be influenced by pub talk? There are decisions being made, even now, by responsible people in calm debate. I'm still hopeful that common sense will prevail.'

'With respect, Mr Hudson,' Frederick said, 'it was you told us yesterday all miners was Reds.'

'They aren't!' Ruby protested, flushing. 'My Uncle Len's a miner, and he's not a Red. He *isn't*, Mr Hudson.'

Hudson, as so often when challenged, fell back upon Higher Authority.

'I gained the information in good faith from Mr Winston Churchill . . . That is to say, quoted in yesterday's newspaper.'

'Peace on earth comes to men of good will,' the actual voice of Higher Authority told them over the crackling wireless waves shortly afterwards, when the phlegmatic Prime Minister, Stanley Baldwin, gave his public reassurance that all would be well. Not much later, the General Strike had begun, and neither peace nor goodwill reigned in Great Britain.

'It really is dreadfully inconsiderate,' Lady Prudence Fairfax pouted. 'I'm giving a dinner party on Wednesday, and they say there'll be no deliveries. And on Saturday I'm going to Wales.'

'There's no chance of that, my dear,' Richard Bellamy told her. 'From midnight tonight trains, buses, all public services come to a grinding halt.'

'Not if we can help it,' Georgina retorted from the morning-room settee, where she sat alongside James. 'We'll drive the trains ourselves. Archie Dunlop's dying to drive a train. He'll take you to Wales, Prue.'

'Does he know the way?'

'Oh, you just point the thing and follow the rails, don't you?'

Lady Prudence shuddered elaborately. 'The thought of any of my friends manning the railways fills me with absolute terror.'

'What happened to the talks last night?' a serious James asked his father above the chatter.

'They ended in confusion. Apparently some *Daily Mail* printers refused to print an article condemning the strike. Baldwin got to hear about it and sent Thomas and company packing. Far too hasty, in my opinion. They were looking to

Baldwin to help them save face. Nobody wants this wretched strike.'

'Well, it's been coming since the end of the war, only people have shut their eyes to it,' James replied morosely. 'What happened in Russia's going to happen here.'

'No one tells me who the fight's between,' Lady Prudence complained. 'The strikers say they're not against the government, but against the mine-owners.'

Richard said, 'It's rather more complicated than that. I don't go so far as James, but there's certainly a strong feeling of solidarity in the working classes – rather like the early days of the war.'

James was on his feet now, the old restlessness re-emerging and causing him to prowl like a pent-up beast.

'Then, we must meet it, Father. We've got law and order on our side. It's intolerable we should be threatened like this.'

His father nodded, though without assurance. 'That's the line Winston's taking. Trade Unions have thrown down the gauntlet. They must suffer the consequences.'

He got up, too.

'Well, I've got to get to the House and see what I can contribute. Ah, Hudson, tell Edward to bring the car round, will you?'

'Yes, my lord,' said the butler, who had just entered. 'I was, er, wondering about her ladyship, my lord. She was to have returned from Inverness tomorrow, but in view of the uncertainty of the trains . . .'

'Good lord, yes! I'll telephone her tonight.'

'Very good. Er, one other thing, my lord . . .'

'Yes?'

'They've been calling on the wireless for volunteers for special constabulary duties. I wondered if I might have your lordship's permission to re-enlist?'

'Of couse, Hudson. Very good idea.'

They left the room together. Georgina turned to James, smiling.

'Will you be volunteering, Jumbo?'

'For what?'

'Anything. I'm going to. Dally says she's going to be a postman. After all, if they won't do the jobs, we've got to do them instead. Then they'll have to give in.'

'Huh! You think they'll just stand by and watch you? You're breaking a strike. Blood will be spilt.'

'In England! What do you suggest we do, then? Drive round in armoured cars?'

Her flippancy was unmatched by James's grim frown and the twitching of his jaw.

'Listen to me, Georgina. A small group of people are quite deliberately trying to cripple our economy. They've forced us to mass our defences, and they might just be misguided enough to fight us all the way. And all you and your friends can do is treat it as some huge lark, to fill the boredom of your empty lives.'

He stamped out of the room from which his so easily exasperated nature had often caused him to stamp.

'Pompous ass!' Georgina said quietly after him.

Virginia was not the only member of the household stranded away from home. Mrs Bridges was at Yarmouth, visiting her sister. She took the momentous step of telephoning Eaton Place to advise the stocking up of food against the shortages she believed to be imminent.

'You seen Eddie?' Daisy asked Frederick, while Mr Hudson and Rose were taking it in turns to try to reassure the absent cook that mass-starvation had not yet manifested itself. 'He's bin gone ages for the milk.'

'Probably having to queue,' Frederick said.

Edward had gone in the car to the emergency centre in Hyde Park. At that moment he came in by the area door, his face red and his nose even more so. Daisy flew to him.

'Eddie! What's happened? You had an accident?'

'All right, Dais, all right. Don't fuss. It's nothing serious.'

'There's blood!' she wailed, and Hudson called, 'Ruby, get some water, quickly!'

Edward sank down at the table, thrusting an already bloodied handkerchief to his nose.

'It was all quite peaceful,' he explained in muffled tones. 'Crowds of people, but I'd just got the milk and back into the car . . . Oh, thanks, Rose.'

After brief ministering he continued.

'I had my sign up in the window, like his lordship told me, saying "Signal for Lift", and this great big bloke comes up, about eight foot tall. He looks in the window, calls me "scab", and then gets hold of my nose and twists it half off my face.'

'He's torn some of the skin off,' said Daisy, peering.

'It's bloody painful, I can tell you. Why pick on me, though?'

Rose explained the obvious. 'You was wearing a chauffeur's uniform and driving a posh car. He thought you should've been striking, too.'

'That's daft,' Frederick interjected. 'I mean, we got no grievances. Have we?'

'No, Frederick, you have not,' Mr Hudson told him firmly. 'And now, I must be off and report for duty.'

He thrust his constable's truncheon into his coat pocket.

'If any hooligan attempts to twist my nose, God help him!'

It was so rarely that Mr Hudson had ever been heard to invoke his Maker that even Edward forgot his distress and watched with as much awe as the rest as the master of their downstairs domain took his leave.

Four days later the nose was still tender, but in the meantime Edward's social conscience had become even more tender.

'You know, Dais,' he ruminated, 'I know it bloody well hurt at the time, but driving round since then, and seeing all those blokes just standing about in groups – bus drivers, engine drivers, and all that, out of work because they're sticking up for the miners – well, it's made me think a bit. I mean, they're only asking for a decent wage.'

'Don't agree with you,' said Frederick, who by this time had been enrolled as a probationary Special and assigned the duty of escort to an omnibus driven by Volunteer Driver Major James Bellamy and conducted by a young Oxford scholar, by name Andrew Bouverie. 'They're disrupting the country,' Frederick went on. 'You can't do that and get away with it.'

As always, Daisy rounded on anyone who did not side with her husband.

'Eddie and me know what it's like to go without a decent wage. There's nothing you can do if nobody'll listen to you.'

Rose asked, 'How do you know they don't listen? You think people like his lordship don't listen?'

'If he listens, why don't he give 'em what they're asking for?'

Frederick said patiently. 'It's not up to him. There's not enough to go round, anyway.'

'Yeh,' Rose agreed. 'And it's not right for you to be talking that way, Daisy. Didn't his lordship come down here yesterday, explaining how all our loyalties was needed not only to this house but to the country? Well, that's a fine way to repay him!'

'Eddie and me's not disloyal!'

'Then show it and shut up, both of you. Every day there's people telling us the strike's all wrong – cleverer people than Edward and you. On the wireless – saying it's wicked and causing misery, and you come out with this drivel! All I can say is, don't let Mr Hudson catch you.'

The bell from the morning-room, where James and his conductor had been refreshing themselves with a drink while their omnibus stood parked incongruously outside in the fashionable thoroughfare, summoned Frederick back to duty. Edward wandered over to his wireless set and switched it on. After the long moments of its warming up they heard the precise tones of an announcer in mid-bulletin.

'. . . that there have been no formal moves towards resumption of negotiations. Mr Baldwin's declaration still stands that the general strike order must be withdrawn before there can be any discussion of peace. To this, so far, the answer of the T.U.C. has been an uncompromising refusal. The Cabinet declares firmly that it cannot discuss terms while any question of intimidation remains.'

'There, see?' Rose said. ' "Intimidation".'

'Meanwhile, it is reported that London has solved most of its traffic problem . . .'

Daisy glanced out of the window. 'There's two people coming down.'

'. . . Omnibus services have steadily increased. Yesterday several hundreds were available, many of them running normal services at a few minutes' interval.'

There was a knocking at the area door. Daisy got up to answer it.

'Cricket,' the announcer was continuing. 'Against Surrey at the Oval the Australians have scored 246 for 6. Taylor made 76 and Woodfull is 60 not out.'

Edward switched off and they heard a man's voice heavily-accented saying to Daisy, 'Be a good lass and tell her her Uncle Len's here, with Mr Thompson from Barnsley.'

Instead, Daisy ushered them in, two stocky, middle-aged men with pale, lean faces under flat caps, which they removed as they entered the servants' hall. Their suits were drab and of rough shoddy cloth.

'Uncle Len!' Ruby exclaimed.

'Hello, Ruby,' one of the men said, smiling with his lips, though not with his tired eyes. 'Just thowt we'd drop in to see thee. Have a piece of cake and a cup o' tea, if there's one going'.'

Introductions were made and tea made and served at the long table. The visitors ate and drank eagerly.

'Come all the way from Yorkshire, have you?' Edward asked.

'That's right, lad,' said Uncle Len. 'Mr Thompson and me's pit delegates for t'Mineworkers' Federation, up for t'big meeting tonight.'

'What are things like in Barnsley?' Rose asked.

'Are you winning?' Edward added.

'Oh, we'll win, right enough. We're fighting for bread, not t'moon. Nobbut a simple living wage.'

'Church says we're right,' Mr Thompson put it. 'Archbishop of Canterbury hisself – only t'wireless won't let 'im broadcast because government says they're not to. Call this a Christian country!'

'Aye,' Uncle Len agreed, 'When they let Winston Churchill

go clattering on about revolution and civil war. It's nobbut a stunt to panic folk.'

'My Eddie got attacked,' Daisy said. Edward fingered his healed but still tender nose.

'Aye, well, a few maybe,' Uncle Len had to admit. 'But most of us, we're peaceful, law-abiding folk.'

Mr Thompson pulled out the newspaper they had seen sticking from his jacket pocket and tossed it on to the table.

'If tha wants truthful picture, take a look at our paper. Most folk don't know nowt about a miner's life. Every five hours a man or boy killed. Nine hundred maimed every day, some for life. You still find skeletons of little lads and lasses down there.'

The servants were staring at the grey men opposite them with incredulity and growing horror.

'And all for what?' Uncle Len took over. 'Fifty-six shillings a week. And now t'owners want to drop it to seven-and-six a shift. Work that out over a five and a half day week. Forty-one shilling, to keep a wife and bairns.'

Edward swallowed. 'We . . . never knew it was like that.'

Uncle Len shrugged. 'We're not asking you to fight our battles.'

'No,' said Mr Thompson, whose voice was harsher and sharpened to a more bitter edge, 'but millions are. Most working folk know we've got a cause.'

The area door opened and closed again with a firmness which the servants knew to be Mr Hudson's particular touch. He entered and surveyed the visitors with surprise. He was less than his immaculate self.

'You bin in a fight, Mr Hudson?' Edward asked.

'A wee scuffle. Two youths, writing seditious slogans on the pavement. I managed to apprehend them both. They won't trouble us again for a while, I fancy.'

'Get Mr Hudson a cup of tea, Ruby,' Rose ordered, then proceeded to introduce their guests. 'They've come up for a miners' delegates' meeting,' she explained finally.

Hudson regarded them with unconcealed distaste.

'I'd have thought the only thing to meet about was to call off this wicked strike,' he said. 'You've gained nothing from it. The country is still on its feet, in spite of your efforts.'

Uncle Len said quietly, 'We've no wish to wreck this country, Mr Hudson.'

'No,' Mr Thompson said less moderately. 'You're the ones wrecking it. Blackleg labour and special constables. Putting young strikers behind bars.'

'It is the duty of every loyal subject to do what he can against the forces of evil who are out to destroy our liberty.'

'Liberty! Oh, you can talk about liberty, living comfortable down here . . .'

'We know what he means,' Uncle Len interrupted his colleague. 'Come on, Arnold. We've out-stayed our welcome. Goodbye, Mr Hudson. It's been instructive meeting you. So long, Ruby, lass. Your Mum'll be glad we dropped by.'

He nodded once in farewell to the rest of them and went out, followed by Thomson, who made no gesture. Mr Hudson sat down to the table, to the tea Ruby had just brought him. He saw the newspaper lying there. Recognition of its title caused him to put down his cup before he had even sipped from it.

'Do you know what that rag is?' he raged. 'It is a seditious propaganda sheet, put out by communists.'

'It isn't, Mr Hudson,' Ruby retorted. 'My uncle Len brought it.'

'You be quiet, girl. I tell you it's printed by traitors, and I forbid a copy of it in this house. Take it out and burn it at once. Rose, I want to talk to you.'

He got to his feet, leaving the tea untouched, and went into his pantry. Rose followed and closed the door. He turned angrily on her.

'You know perfectly well that you are responsible here when I am absent. I can see it isn't safe to leave this house for a moment, though.'

'What d'you mean, Mr Hudson?'

'Those two miners you saw fit to entertain are the very sort of people we're fighting . . .'

'It's Ruby's uncle! I couldn't turn him away.'

'You could, and should have, as a duty to this household. Have you no intelligence, girl. This is the house of a prominent member of the government. Things are spoken here and written down that could be of immense value to the wrong people.'

'They're not spies, Mr Hudson.'

'They're enemies and traitors.'

'They're not! They're Englishmen, same as us. They're not enjoying the strike any more'n we are. At least we can treat 'em with a bit of civility.'

'Calm down, Rose, calm down. All I'm trying to point out to you is that feelings on both sides are running high at the moment. It's up to the saner ones amongst us to cut out any loose talk that could unbalance people like Edward and Daisy and Ruby. It's up to us to set an example of responsibility and loyalty. Do you understand, Rose?'

Less than convinced, she could only nod.

'Very well, Rose. We'll say no more about it.'

He ushered her out and followed her, to return to his teacup.

Mr Hudson was not the only man in Britain who feared the direct consequences his country might suffer from the General Strike. Many who had sympathised with the miners on sheer humanitarian grounds had begun to grow alarmed by reports – both true and false – of rabble-rousing, damage and personal violence. A High Court judge upheld Sir John Simon's denunciation of the strike as illegal, causing law-respecting Unionists to re-examine their views and bringing nearer the likelihood of widespread arrests and active intervention by the armed forces, who so far had been used principally only for escorting convoys of vital supplies and protecting volunteers in the public services from attack.

No lives had been lost through direct violence, but there had been many scuffles, injuries and arrests. The derailment of the Flying Scotsman express train by strikers near Newcastle shocked and outraged the nation.

In the Trades Union Congress headquarters in Eccleston Square, moderate leaders grew increasingly alarmed at evidence of foreign moves to manipulate the striking workers into violent confrontation with the forces of law and order and to accomplish a political revolution. It began to appear to some onlookers that the T.U.C. were doing more than the government to bring the strike to an end.

'Over a week now!' Richard Bellamy exclaimed to James as they sat over evening brandies in the morning-room. 'Baldwin claims to be the man of peace and sits back doing nothing.'

'What can he do, Father? The strike notices are still up.'

'There are plenty of things he can do. He can bring people together in private – mine-owners, Union leaders, and anyone else with something to offer. He can listen to them, discuss with them; listen to members of his own party. Men with vision and vast experience. Last night I was with Reading and Wimbourne, two ex-viceroys, and a few others. We sat up half the night, drafted several schemes, presented them to Baldwin this morning – and he hasn't even acknowledged them. I'm not saying we have the answer, but at least we're trying every way to find it.'

'But why compromise at all? We're winning. We're proving that, the longer it goes on.'

'The longer it goes on, James, the worse will be the consequences. The war of attrition will be absolutely disastrous.'

James shook his head emphatically. 'We've got them on the run. Why let them escape?'

Georgina had come into the room in time to hear him.

'They're beaten already,' she said. 'They're saying the country has let them down.'

'They can't blame the country,' James persisted. 'It's their own leaders they should blame. Defy them and get back to work.'

Richard disagreed, 'If they defy their leadership, it's the end of the Trade Unions. The country must have Trade Unions.'

'Not with leaders who've been discredited. They've committed a criminal act and they must be punished.'

Georgina, weary from a trip to Manchester and back that day in the care of a young man-about-town, delivering a consignment of the government published newspaper, the *British Gazette*, flared up at this.

'Why do you always have to talk like that, James? Always about punishment . . . and war. People don't want to hear about it any more. They just want to be left in peace, with enough to eat, to enjoy themselves.'

She turned back to the door.

'I'm exhausted. I'm going to bed. Goodnight, Uncle Richard.'

But even as this brief clash took place, talks were going on elsewhere which would bring the strike to its end. Sir Herbert Samuel, who had been away in Italy had returned – driven from Dover to London by the racing motorist Sir Henry Seagrave as if to symbolise the urgency of his return – and plunged at once into secret negotiations with the T.U.C. The miners' leaders were carefully not consulted.

At No. 165 Eaton Place next day, Richard spoke into the morning-room telephone, watched by his son.

'Yes, yes. It's splendid news. Thank you for telephoning. Goodbye.'

He replaced the receiver and turned to James.

'The end's in sight. The T.U.C. leaders are at Downing Street now. They've agreed to call off the strike so that negotiations with the miners can begin. It should be over within the hour.'

'J. H. Thomas has accepted Samuel's formula?'

'That's it.'

'Well, he may have done, but what about the miners?'

'They must accept, too. They've no choice left. You don't look particularly pleased, James.'

'Yes, I'm pleased, Father. Just wondering what happens when we've all finished congratulating ourselves.'

Richard regarded him with little surprise. Little ever seemed to gratify James. Nothing did wholly.

'There'll be no vindictiveness from this government,' Richard answered. 'Baldwin has given his word on that. The industry will be reorganised. All strikers will be reinstated without penalty. Don't you see, James, we've kept our civil liberty. Our greatest asset.'

James nodded, but said morosely, 'A campaign fought with a mass of guns – against a pathetic, futile enemy.'

Richard raised his shoulders and let them sag as he expelled his breath in a sigh.

'Ah, well . . . If you won't join me in a drink to victory, at least take one to avoidance of defeat.'

He went to ring for Hudson and champagne.

'Going to miss your constable duties, Mr Hudson?' Frederick asked some time later.

'Not a bit, Frederick. It gives me no pleasure chasing hooligans at my age, I can assure you.'

Edward said, 'Bit of a let-down, now it's all over. No more bloody battles in the street.'

'No more getting your nose tweaked,' Daisy reminded him, tapping it lightly, causing him to wince away.

Rose was over by the wireless set, trying to tune it finely, frowning as she concentrated against the background conversation. Ruby stood puckering her brow, fiddling doubtfully with the hem of her apron.

'Will they get more money?' she asked suddenly. Everyone except Rose looked at her inquiringly. 'Miners,' she explained. 'Will they get more?'

'Course they will,' Edward assured her. 'Your Uncle Len and all of 'em. Won't they, Mr Hudson?'

'I, er . . . From what I can gather they'll get . . . the same, at any rate, Ruby.

'Listen!' Rose exclaimed from across the room. The final bars of the National Anthem crackled over the ether.

They listened in silence until it ended. Hudson looked at his watch.

'Right,' he addressed them all briskly. 'Now back to your duties, everybody. We have allowed things to become very slipshod in this household, these past nine days. It behoves us to follow the example of the nation as a whole and return to our work with a will.'

He strode pantry-wards. Exchanging a variety of glances, the rest obediently began to move their separate ways.

CHAPTER TWO

As he came down the stairs into the hall of No. 165, carrying a breakfast tray, Mr Hudson suddenly grimaced. He paused on his way towards the kitchen stairs and laid the tray on a side table, to free himself to massage his left arm with his right. The pain he had just felt there had been sudden and intense.

As he continued to rub the still throbbing arm he heard the morning-room bell ringing distantly. Hudson would never have allowed personal discomfort to come before duty. He adjusted his cuffs, straightened his back, and went in. He found Lord Bellamy, the Major and Miss Georgina, evidently comparing diaries.

'Ah, Hudson. The French Ambassador's coming to dinner. Monsieur Fleuriau. Friday the sixteenth.'

'Very good, my lord.'

Hudson could feel the onset of new pain, but he stood impassively, hearing James say, 'Sorry, Father, can't manage. Playing polo. Shan't be in any sort of form for ambassadors after six chukkers at Cowdray.'

Georgina said, 'And I've been invited sailing at Bembridge that weekend.'

'But I was counting on you both!' Lord Bellamy protested.

Hudson ventured, 'Will her ladyship not have returned from Scotland, my lord?'

'Yes, she returns on Monday. She'll be here.'

'There you are, then,' James said. 'You don't need us.'

'But I do. I want Georgina to bring her own special charm to the occasion . . .'

'Thank you, Uncle Richard.'

'. . . and you to take care of the Fleuriau daughter.'

'How old?'

'Well, er, about sixteen.'

'Steady on, Father!'

They laughed. Hudson felt himself beginning to perspire.

'Well,' James said, shutting his little diary with a snap, 'it shouldn't be too hard to think of someone. I'm sorry, Father, but . . .'

Mr Hudson suddenly knew he had to get out of the room quickly. For once in his life he interrupted.

'Will it be eight for dinner, my lord?'

Three surprised faces looked at him.

'Yes, Hudson, eight,' Lord Bellamy said. 'You can tell Mrs Bridges to start thinking it over before her ladyship returns.'

'Yes, my lord.'

'You . . . all right, Hudson?'

'Quite all right, thank you, my lord.'

All the same, he was glad to get beyond the door and even allowed himself to sit on a hall chair for some moments before taking up the tray again and going slowly down the kitchen stairs.

He felt normal again by supper time, but he merely picked at the food on his plate.

'You going to give them your French cuisine, Mrs Bridges?' Daisy asked.

'I don't know yet. Depends on her ladyship.' An afterthought struck her. 'I never given French cuisine to a Frenchman before.'

'Expect they'd like something simple for a change,' Frederick said. 'Good old Yorkshire pud.'

'Yeh, and Ruby's apple dumplings,' Edward supported him. 'I bet your dumplings is famous at the French Embassy, Ruby.'

'Why ever should they?'

'Mr Hudson knows the butler there, don't you, Mr Hudson? Bound to've told him.'

'Ed's only teasing,' Daisy said. 'You know him, Ruby.'

But the exchange had drawn Mrs Bridges' attention to Mr Hudson's neglect of his plate. She frowned and became the second person that day to ask if he was feeling all right. He murmured an untrue apology about having had two large slices of bread and jam at teatime and lost his appetite. He gave them all a reassuring smile; but he was feeling vaguely uncomfortable about the arm and chest. He retired to bed before any of the others, and was thankful to do so.

'What's that you're reading?' Daisy asked Frederick.

'A book.'

'I can see it's a book. What about?'

'Not for little girls.'

Rose leaned over the back of his chair and grabbed it playfully.

'It's about wine,' she announced, surprised.

'That's right. Mr Hudson lent it me.'

'What do you want to know about wine for?'

'I'm interested, that's why.' He seized the book back. 'It's a footman's duty to know about things.'

'Not wine,' Rose argued. 'That's a butler's duty.'

'Yeah, well . . . I'm not going to be a footman all my life, am I?'

Edward came in. Daisy told him, 'Fred's learning up about wine.'

Edward shrugged. 'I know about wine. Give us a question, Fred.'

Without consulting the book, and wearing the look of supercilious amusement which Ruby secretly thought highly romantic, Frederick complied.

'Where are the Saint-Emilion wines grown?'

'Not that kind of question,' Edward said. 'You don't have to know where they're grown.'

Frederick's dark humour increased.

'Right,' he accepted. 'Give us the names of four different clarets.'

'Clarets? Er . . . Chauteau, er . . . Chateau, er . . .'

'Latour, Lafite, Margaux, Haut-Brion . . . Got a long way to go to catch me up,' Frederick said smugly, getting to his feet and stretching. 'So long.' He went off to bed, leaving Edward and Daisy affronted and the others impressed.

A small crisis hit the household a few mornings later. It came in the form of a telephone call from Virginia, to say that an outbreak of mumps had occurred in the Scottish village she was visiting. She herself was feverish and had been ordered to bed by the doctor. He was unsure whether she had caught the complaint, but was being adamant that she must not travel to London in time for the dinner party.

'Postpone it,' Georgina told Richard. He shook his head. She knew enough of the niceties of diplomatic relations to be aware that one didn't disrupt an ambassador's forward planning, but adopted emergency measures to ensure that those plans went smoothly and agreeably.

'Ah, well,' she said. 'To avoid a diplomatic incident I'll cancel Bembridge. I'm not awfully fond of sailing, anyway.'

Richard thanked her warmly. His look of relief made up her mind for her, and she sought out James to tell him it was his duty to help in the backing-up operation. At length he raised his hands in a mock gesture of surrender and they summoned Mrs Bridges to the morning-room.

'The most important thing,' James prepared his cousin as they awaited her coming, 'is not to let her bully you. Ah, Mrs Bridges, do come in. We thought we should discuss this menu.'

'Yes, sir,' their small but formidable cook replied. 'I was thinking of a saddle of lamb.'

'Oh, ah, you were? Well, all right. Plenty of garlic . . .'

'Not too much, sir. And my onion sauce, if you think that's suitable.'

'Oh, yes. Fine. Now, the soup. Mulligatawny?'

'Mock turtle, sir. Followed by fillet of sole à la Colbert and my vol-au-vents of oysters.'

James opened his mouth to attempt some slight modification, but Mrs Bridges sailed on.

'After the lamb, partridge.'

'Oh!' James managed. 'Had my fill of partridge lately. Can't it be grouse?'

Mrs Bridges crushed him with a firm shake of her grey head.

'The partridges from Southwold are just about ready, sir. With one of my salads, of course. Then sorbets. Meringue or

Peach Melba to follow, and perhaps an apricot soufflé.'

James turned to Georgina, annoyed to find her smirking at him.

'How does that sound to you?' he asked, hoping she would over-rule some detail, but was annoyed to hear her say, 'Lovely!'

James accepted defeat with abrupt courtesy to the cook, who left them, quite under the impression that she had just received orders for the dinner party from the master of the house.

As ill luck would have it, Mr Hudson felt, the evening of the dinner coincided with a harsh return of the symptoms he had been feeling from time to time recently. In pain and perspiring copiously, he found it impossible to move briskly about his duties. His distress was exacerbated by what he took for nagging on the part of the other male servants.

'Haven't you opened the wine yet, Mr Hudson? I'll do it for you, if you like.'

'Cocktails are all ready in the drawing-room, Mr Hudson. The fire's made up.'

'His lordship's clothes is all laid out. Just waiting for the Major to call me.'

'Frederick!' he exploded. 'Your shoes are squeaking. Take them off and soften them up.'

'But I bought them special, Mr Hudson.'

'There is nothing more intolerable at a dinner party than a footman with squeaking shoes. Go on, now. No, wait. Is the drawing-room ready?'

'I just told you.'

Rose bustled in with a necklace in her hands.

'An enormous great bunch of flowers has just come from her ladyship to wish Miss Georgina luck,' she reported excitedly. 'Mr Hudson, can you get this necklace of Miss Georgina's unfastened? I can't.'

Hudson made no answer, but turned away, his head reeling. Frederick took the necklace from Rose and began to fiddle with its clasp himself.

In his pantry, Hudson mopped his brow yet again and slowly went about the suddenly laborious business of changing into his evening dress and white tie.

'Mr Hudson's in a funny mood,' Rose remarked to Mrs Bridges. 'Looks all hot and bothered.'

'Yes, well I'm all hot and bothered, with the help I'm getting. Oh, Ruby, where's the stewpan got to now?'

'Just behind you, Mrs Bridges.'

'Well, give it here, then.'

And so it continued for half an hour longer, until it occurred to Rose that she had better give Mr Hudson a knock and remind him that it was approaching seven-thirty. He had not emerged from his pantry, and both Edward and Frederick had kept glancing uneasily at the six unopened bottles of Chateau Latour 1906, waiting for him to reappear and draw the corks.

He answered her knock with the impatient reply that he would be out in a minute. Rose was just turning to go when there came a crash from within the pantry which reached the ears of the others in the hall. As they moved towards her, their expressions registering puzzlement and alarm, Rose knocked harder on the door and called Mr Hudson's name. This time there was no response.

Rose jerked open the door and went in. Hudson was lying almost at her feet, his body jerking in pain, one hand clutching his chest, his lips drawn back as he gasped fiercely for breath.

'Mrs Bridges!' Rose cried. 'Fetch Mrs Bridges somebody.'

But Mrs Bridges was already approaching, wiping her hands on her apron. She took one look and ordered, 'Rose – telephone for the doctor. Quick!'

Rose hurried to obey. Frederick asked, 'What about the dinner?'

'Never mind the dinner,' the cook replied, getting down on her knees beside the prone man. 'Go and tell 'em upstairs there may be a bit of delay.'

She lowered her mouth close to Hudson's ear. He was making little moaning sounds, trying to speak.

'It's all right, Angus,' she told him. 'It's Kate here. You had a fall, that's all. It's all right, dear.'

Edward, Daisy and Ruby watched petrified as she cradled him, stroking his hair like a child's. He was silent now, his eyes closed, and he lay inertly against her. He looked as if he were dead.

Dr Foley was round within minutes. While he examined Hudson in the privacy of the butler's pantry, the rest tried to concentrate on preparations for the dinner party. It was not easy.

'Sauce is ready, Mrs Bridges,' Ruby reported.

'I can't think about sauces!'

'You must,' Rose intervened. 'Now come on, taste it and see if Ruby's done it right.'

She thrust a spoonful at Mrs Bridges as though force-feeding a child. The cook admitted it to her mouth then spluttered dramatically. 'Garlic! Full of garlic.'

Tears started to Ruby's eyes as she protested, 'I only rubbed the bowl with it, Mrs Bridges – like you told me.'

'It's ruined.'

Rose had tasted it meanwhile. 'No it isn't. It's just right, Ruby. Frenchmen like garlic, anyway. Now is the soup coming on all right?'

'Is it his heart, d'you think?' Mrs Bridges was asking. 'Pray God it isn't his heart. Oh, dear, I'll have to sit down a minute.'

Rose guided her onto a chair and fetched a glassful of the cooking brandy. 'Just you drink that,' she half-ordered. 'It'll buck you up. And don't you stare, Ruby. Get stirring that soup. Mr Hudson wouldn't want the dinner spoiled because of him.'

Through in the servants' hall a debate was taking place. The participants were Frederick, Edward and Daisy. There was an abrasive edge to the voice of each.

'Who's it goin' to be, then?' Frederick had asked, jerking his head meaningfully towards the pantry.

'My Eddie, of course,' Daisy said at once. 'He was footman here long before you was.'

'I'm footman now. Edward's chauffeur. Footman's next in line, strictly speaking.'

'Don't let's argue about it,' Edward pleaded. 'Let his lordship decide.'

'No, Eddie, you stand up for your rights. They'll be here in twenty minutes, an' you've got to be ready to do butler duties by then. Never mind what he says . . .'

The argument was cut short by the emergence of the elderly, balding Dr Foley from the pantry. He closed the door behind him. His expression was inscrutable.

'It's important he stays resting and has no excitement,' was all the information he gave them. 'This dinner party is rather on his mind, but I insist no one must disturb him. Is that quite clear? I'm going up to see Lord Bellamy now.'

He went away up the stairs, neither Edward nor Frederick thinking to hurry ahead to show him to his lordship's presence. They merely went mechanically about their preparations, glancing frequently at the closed pantry door and wondering what the situation was behind it.

'It's rather serious, Lord Bellamy,' Foley said, his glance embracing James and Georgina, too. All were in evening dress in the drawing-room. The grandfather clock showed a mere twenty minutes to go before the guests were due.

'It is a heart attack. Quite mild, but there's always the danger of a second one following. I don't want to move him tonight. My concern is that he's worrying about his duties.'

'Uncle Richard, we must cancel,' Georgina urged. 'If you telephone there's just time.'

The doctor saved Richard from reminding her that such a move could not be countenanced. 'In some ways,' he pointed out, 'it might be better to carry on as normally as possible, or he'll feel he's let the side down and worry more.'

'I agree,' James said, with a promptness that almost shocked Georgina. She turned to her uncle, but recognised his familiar look of relief whenever spared having to make the vital decision in a crisis.

Dr Foley said, 'There's nothing more I can do just now. I'll be round first thing in the morning – unless there's any change, of course, in which case, please call me at once.'

He went out. The three looked at one another.

'Well,' James said. 'All we can do is depute Edward or Frederick to buttle, and hope for the best.' He pressed the bell. 'Which of them do we choose?'

'Eddie!' Daisy alerted her husband when the bell sounded in the servants' hall. But Frederick was already at the foot of the stairs. 'I'll go,' he said, and did.

Daisy gave Edward an exasperated shake.

'What's the matter with you? I'll tell you this. If they decide on Frederick, they can say goodbye to me in this house. You, too, if you've got any pride. They're not goin' to trample over us.'

But when Frederick returned, very shortly afterwards, he wore a grim look and announced, 'It's you they want.'

Edward's eyes widened with apprehension. Daisy gave him a little shove. 'Think so, as well. Go on, Eddie.'

Edward obediently went up the stairs, watched sardonically by Frederick.

'Don't push him too hard, Dais,' he advised. 'He might fall over one day.'

In the morning-room, Edward received his instructions from Lord Bellamy, conscious of the watchful attention of the Major and Miss Georgina.

'When you bring them into the drawing-room you'll announce them as His Excellency the French Ambassador, Madame Fleuriau and Mademoiselle Fleuriau. Have you got that?'

Edward tried the name and was relieved to get it right.

'Good. And our other two guests are Lord and Lady Swanbourne. You must announce them as the Earl and Countess of Swanbourne.'

'Yes, my lord.'

'Wine's the most important thing,' the Major said. 'Does he know what we're having?'

Richard shot his son a glance of disapproval for having spoken in this third-person way, as if Edward were not even in the room. In the brief discussion over the choice of Hudson's understudy, James had favoured Frederick, but had been outvoted. He could see that the servant was having to rack his memory. He explained carefully, 'We're having Amontillado with the turtle soup. Then champagne to follow – the Moët and Chandon Dry Imperial.'

'That's all ready, my lord,' Edward said thankfully.

'Good. And the claret is the Chateau Latour '06.'

James put in, 'And a Trocken Beeren Auslese with the sorbet.'

Edward had not been told about this last. He committed it to memory without having to admit the deficiency.

'The carving, Edward,' Georgina said, smiling encouragingly. 'You can manage saddle of lamb, I'm sure.'

'Oh, yes, miss. I've carved several times when Hudson's . . . been away.'

'You'll manage splendidly,' Richard smiled. It was James again who, characteristically, struck a chord of uncertainty.

'Will he fit into Hudson's black coat?'

'His black coat, sir?' Edward queried, bringing himself into direct communication.

'Well, you can hardly buttle in chauffeur's uniform, can you?'

Richard said firmly, 'I think you're roughly Hudson's height and build, aren't you?'

'Just about, m'lord.'

'Well, you'd better go and get ready. We haven't much time.'

'Very good, my lord.'

Georgina asked, 'How's Mrs Bridges?'

'Well . . . rather upset, miss.'

'I'm sure. One of us would have come down, only we don't want to get in the way just now.'

'Yes, miss. She's carrying on all right – with Ruby's help, and Rose's.'

'Wish her luck,' Richard told him. 'And good luck to you, Edward.'

'Thank you, m'lord – Miss Georgina.'

He felt no temptation to thank the Major, as well.

'You didn't exactly give him confidence,' Georgina snapped at James, when the servant had gone.

'Now, now,' Richard ruled. 'No arguments, please. I've no fears at all. Some of Hudson's influence must have rubbed off on him in all this time. I'm sure he'll come through with flying colours.'

James's lack of encouragement above stairs was matched by Frederick's below.

'Bit of a loose fit, eh?' he commented, watching Daisy tightening the strap of Hudson's waistcoat to its utmost to make the garment fit her husband more snugly.

'Looks better than it would on you,' she retorted. 'Great beanpole!'

Unabashed, Frederick said casually, ''Bout time you uncorked the wine, isn't it, Edward? Want to get some air at it. I'll do it.'

'No, I'll do the wine,' Edward said, with rare determination.

'Yes. He'll do it,' Daisy echoed, still struggling with the waitscoat. 'Oh, Eddie, do stand still.'

But he almost jumped in the air as the front door bell sounded.

'Cor! They're here, and I'm not ready yet.'

Rose came through from the kitchen, hissing, 'Shush! Keep your voices down. He's only next door, remember.'

They all glanced at the pantry door. Behind it, Hudson, conscious of the agitated murmurs, stirred anxiously.

With the authority of her longer service, Rose ordered, 'You go up, Frederick. You go with him, Dais. I'll finish helping Eddie. Go *on*!'

The two went obediently. Edward wailed, 'He won't know the right announcin', Rose. Oh, blimey! An' the blinkin' wine's not opened yet, and I'll have to be in the drawing-room serving cocktails. Oh . . . !'

'Stand still and let me do your tie. Fred'll do the cocktails, and there's half an hour before dinner. Plenty of time for the wine to air. There. You look fine.'

As it transpired, the arrivals had been Lord and Lady Swanbourne. By the time the doorbell rang again, Edward was ready to open it to the Ambassadorial family.

'Good evening, your Excellency,' he said, with a bow.

The Ambassador was middle-aged, small and elegantly slim. His eyes twinkled good-humouredly and he replied in excellent English.

'Good evening. Am I right? Is it Hudson?'

'No, your Excellency.'

'No? But my own butler told me I was meeting the famous Hudson this evening.'

'Hudson is . . . indisposed, your Excellency. I . . . I'm Barnes.'

If Fleuriau was disappointed he was too good a diplomat to show it. When Frederick and Daisy had taken their coats, Edward led the guests up to the drawing-room and made the introductions with accuracy and aplomb.

Back in the lower regions, Frederick soon deflated his self-satisfaction. He indicated the bottles of claret, now uncorked.

'You do know that's best claret, Edward?'

'So what?'

'I mean, you wasn't going to serve it like that, surely?'

'It's having enough time to breathe. Air temperature.'

Frederick said pityingly, 'Best Chateau Latour – from the bottle! It wants decanting.'

'Decanting? His lordship didn't say nothing about decanting.'

'Expected you'd know, that's why. Daisy, fetch some decanters, quick.'

She gave him a glare, but obeyed. She offered a decanter to Edward on her return, but Frederick took it.

'I'll do it. Needs a steady hand, or the deposit'll be disturbed. You go up and pour the champagne.'

Edward hesitated. Daisy opened her mouth to protest, but managed to restrain her anger when she saw the concentration Frederick was already applying to the delicate task. Edward had no alternative but to obey the order from his temporary underling.

Despite the disruption of the ordered way of things; despite the rivalry, the jealousy and the sporadic outbursts of bickering; despite Mrs Bridges' distraction; despite even a dramatic appearance by Hudson, ghost-like in pyjamas, who had to be hustled back to bed and reassured that they were coping all right; despite all these difficulties, the evening seemed to have been a success. The plates came down cleared, the bottles and decanters all but emptied. Nothing was spilt, nor overlooked, nor wrongly timed.

When the guests had at last departed, Georgina came to the kitchen, where washing up and putting away were interrupted for her to address them all.

'I just want to thank you for the wonderful job you did tonight. I was nervous. It was the first time I'd been hostess for such a distinguished dinner, but I needn't have worried, it seems. The Ambassador was delighted. He complimented every course, Mrs Bridges.'

'Very kind of you to tell me, miss. Rose and Ruby was a great help.'

'I'm sure they were. Thank you both, too. And Edward, I know his lordship was as pleased as I was at the way you handled everything.'

'Thank you, miss.'

'Frederick and Daisy . . . all of you, you did Hudson proud. Thank you most sincerely. Goodnight.'

They chorused their thanks. Awake in his bed, Hudson heard the sound and identified it. He knew that all had gone well, after all. It did not bring him full relief, though. He felt suddenly that, in his absence, things had no business to go without a hitch. He felt out of it and forgotten already.

'Six months' complete rest at least,' was Dr Foley's verdict to Richard and Georgina after he had seen his patient again next morning. 'I don't want to move him for a week or so, but I think it's important he should go away from here.'

Richard asked, 'Frankly, what are his chances of recovery?'

'Oh, there's no reason why he shouldn't get over it.'

'And return to his duties?'

'In time. But he must change his ways. Take proper rests in

the afternoon. No heavy lifting. Delegate some of his responsibilities.'

'He'll hate that,' Georgina said.

'I gather he's a stubborn fellow, but he must learn to live with it or risk the consequences. He'll be his own worst enemy unless he has the firmest handling.'

'Come in, Mrs Bridges,' Richard called, as there came a knock at the morning-room door. As Hudson's most senior colleague and known friend, the cook had been summoned to represent downstairs in the appraisal of the situation. Her eyes widened with alarm when Richard told her the doctor's pronouncement.

'No, not for ever,' he hastened to reassure her. 'Just a few months, for a complete rest. Now, have you any ideas where he might go? I was wondering about his sister in Hastings.'

'Well, my lord, I do know she suffers dreadful with arthritis these days. Finds it hard to manage her guest home.'

Dr Foley shook his head. 'He's going to need some careful nursing.'

Mrs Bridges' eyes lit up. 'There's his old friends down at Southwold, my lord. Mr and Mrs Trantor. She's the village postmistress and I think she did a bit of nursing in the war.'

'He'll be an invalid for some time,' the doctor said. 'It would be quite an undertaking for them. Do you think they could manage?'

'Oh, I'm sure they could. They're kind souls and have been very fond of Hudson since he was a young footman at the House. I know they've kept up regular correspondence, my lord.'

'I seem to remember them. They sound ideal. I'll write to them. Thank you, Mrs Bridges.'

She hesitated. 'He . . . will get better, my lord, won't he? I couldn't bear to think . . .'

Dr Foley took her gently by the arm and led her to the door.

'He was one of the lucky ones, Mrs Bridges,' he told her. 'He'll be all right.'

She went downstairs much relieved and dispensed the news

to the others. After the initial reaction of relief, it provoked almost predictable events.

A little later that morning, Frederick was glad to find the excuse he had been seeking to have a word alone with his former officer. James had sent him out for some tobacco. He delivered it to James in his own room, then lingered.

'Anything else, sir?'

'Not at the moment.'

Frederick still waited.

'How are things downstairs?'

'Bit unsettled really, sir. We just heard Hudson's going to be away quite a while.'

'So I gather. You'll manage, won't you? The dinner seemed to go off all right.'

'Thank you, sir. Apart from the mix-up about the claret . . .'

'What was that? I didn't notice anything.'

'We, er, managed to cover it up, fortunately.'

'What happened?'

'Well, it's all over now, sir . . .'

'No, come on. Tell me.'

'It was just . . . I noticed Edward about to serve the claret straight from the bottle. Luckily, I . . .'

There came a knock at the door and Daisy entered, carrying bed-linen. James waved her through to his bedroom. As she went she heard him say, 'Not decanted, eh?'

'Well, it was in the end, sir. Luckily I noticed in time. He had a lot of things on his mind, after all, sir.'

'Very sharp of you, Frederick. Terrible blunder to have served our best claret straight from the bottle.'

Daisy glanced back through the open door, seething inwardly at Frederick's smug smirk as he replied, 'Specially to a Frenchman, sir.'

'To anyone,' she heard the Major say. 'You an expert on these matters, Frederick?'

'Wouldn't say an expert . . .'

'Don't be modest. Very useful knowledge for someone in your position who wants to make his way in the world. Ever feel you're dragging your heels a bit, do you? Been here – what? – seven years. Want to move on?'

Frederick answered carefully, 'I'd be very sad to leave your employment, sir. I've always been very happy here . . . and there was the war.'

'Mm. But you don't want to go to waste, do you? Got resource, ambition.'

'I look at the future sometimes, sir.'

'And wonder what it holds for you, eh?'

'Yes, sir.'

James had finished filling his pipe. He gave Frederick a thoughtful glance, before saying dismissively, 'All right, *Trooper* Norton.' Frederick's purpose had not escaped him.

Daisy had never made a bed so savagely in her life.

'Don't you try denyin' it,' she accused Frederick as soon as she could get down to the servants' hall to confront him. 'You brought it up deliberate, just to make Eddie look stupid. I know your game.'

'Leave it, Dais,' her husband requested mildly.

'That's right, Ed,' said Frederick. 'You want to stop your wife puffing and blowing, or she's going to get me angry.'

This was too much even for Edward.

'Now just a minute. She's entitled to speak her mind. Strikes me what you did was pretty underhand. I wouldn't've done it to you, so don't you start on her. You tell me if you got anything to say.'

'I got nothing to say to you. I got no grudge – but she keeps on at me.'

'No grudge?' Daisy flamed. 'No grudge, when you go suckin' up to the Major, tellin' tales . . .'

'Shut up, you silly cow!' he yelled back, causing her to catch her breath and fall silent. 'Sorry, Eddie,' he said quickly, 'but I did warn you.' But Daisy was too far gone in fury to heed him.

'Yeh – and you bin suckin' up to Mr Hudson these past weeks, too. Don't think I haven't noticed, with your fancy wine book.'

'Oh, yeh. I knew he was going to have a heart attack, so I

started telling nasty tales about Edward.'

Edward pleaded with them both. 'Shut up, will you? For pity's sake. Look, I know my worth in this household. It's up to them upstairs to decide anything.'

Daisy turned on him. 'Someone's got to do your talkin', Eddie. You'll never do it yourself. You're older, you've been here longer, and you was a corporal in the war and he was only a trooper. You know you're the better man.'

'But I saw the war out, didn't I?' Frederick demanded viciously. '*And* I was here when they took you back on sufferance.'

'You – dirty – pig!' Daisy breathed, half stunned. 'If I was a man, I'd box your head in for that. Eddie, you're lettin' him walk all over you and doin' nothin' . . .'

Rose stormed in. 'What's all this shouting? You're making enough noise to waken the . . . What's going on?'

'Just a private discussion,' Frederick said impassively.

'About who's takin' over – my Eddie or . . .'

'Nobody's taking over anything,' Rose told Daisy angrily. 'You give me the pip, you lot do. There's poor Mr Hudson lying there fighting for his life, and you lot got him buried already. It's disgustin'. I'm disgusted with the lot of you!'

She swept out again, leaving them quelled and uneasy.

All the same, Daisy, in her turn, took her chance when it came later that morning.

'Can you take this to the post, Daisy?' Georgina asked, and licked the gum of the envelope she had just addressed at the morning-room desk. 'It's to thank her ladyship for sending the flowers.'

'Yes, miss. How is her ladyship, miss?'

'Oh, much better. It wasn't mumps at all, apparently. Just a bad cold. I'll be very relieved when she gets back.'

'Well, it'll be easier for us all when . . .'

'When she gets back? Don't say you think I'm not coping, Daisy.'

'Oh, no, miss. I meant . . . well, when Hudson's successor's been announced.'

'But Edward's managing, isn't he?'

'Yes, miss. Only, I think he'd just like to know for certain if . . . if the job's his. I mean, on a temporary basis, of course.'

'I assumed it was.'

'He hasn't been told anything definite, and Frederick seems to think he's got rights to it. It's led to a bit of bad feeling.'

Rose entered the room, carrying a coat of Georgina's on to which she had re-sewn a button and was just in time to hear Daisy conclude. 'Not that I've got anything against Frederick, miss . . .'

Rose withered Daisy with a look. Georgina saw it and said, 'Rose, Daisy was just saying . . .'

'I know what she was saying, miss,' Rose said between her teeth. 'And I wouldn't listen to a word of it, if I was you.'

'But is there really bad feeling downstairs?'

'Yes, there is, miss. They're like jackals, Frederick and Edward, both of them. I know it's none of my business, but I don't think either of them deserve the job. We should get in a proper temporary butler while Hudson's away, and teach 'em both a lesson. When I think of all he's done for them over the years it makes my blood boil.'

Georgina stared at this vehemence. Daisy was glad to slip quietly from the room.

While this unrest seethed about him, Mr Hudson lay still, as he had been instructed by Dr Foley, and contemplated his future. He did not like what he saw. For so many years he had been the upholder of the *status quo* in that household, his name known in all the grand homes of Belgravia and well beyond as synonymous with the old standards; the days when servants were servants and masters were masters, and the demarcation lines between them were as clearly drawn as they were between the different degrees of society above stairs and of status below them.

For years – through war, national upheaval, domestic crisis – he had, he fancied not incorrectly, been the principal stabilising influence on those closest to him, and not a little upon those whom he served. And now, ironically, he suddenly found himself helpless, impotent, aware from what he had overheard through his door that his very elimination had brought about a breach in relationships which might never be healed and which might preface the end of the story of the Bellamy household.

He unburdened himself miserably to his one regular visitor, Kate Bridges, as she sat at his bedside and held his hand.

'I feel so lost, Kate. All these years, and to finish up like this.'

'It's *not* finished, Angus. Dr Foley said you were one of the lucky ones, so long as you're careful and take things easy.'

'Lucky? Kate . . . if anything should . . . happen . . .'

'Oh, don't say that!'

'No, no. One must face these things. I just want to tell you that some time ago I arranged to leave all my possessions, such as they are, to you.'

She only just managed not to cry. She had cried so often lately.

'Thank you, Angus. I appreciate that. I've . . . done the same for you.'

He seemed surprised. 'Oh! Thank you. Well . . . there's a little money, and some gold cufflinks his lordship gave me after twenty-five years' service. You can sell them.'

'I couldn't. Never!'

'If times ever get hard . . .'

'I could never sell anything of yours, Angus.'

'Don't cry,' he pleaded. 'Is . . . everything going all right? Without me?'

'No,' she admitted wretchedly. 'It's all topsy-turvy.'

'But Rose told me what a success the dinner was.'

Mrs Bridges remembered that he was not to be worried. All she could find to say was, 'They seem pleased upstairs. You have a nap now. I'll come and see you again this evening.'

She went out and left him staring at the ceiling; ill and concerned.

Upstairs, his office, if not himself, was the subject of further argument.

Richard was saying, 'We mustn't judge Edward simply on the matter of the claret.'

'No,' James conceded. 'But you must agree that a butler's principal function is knowledge of the cellar; and Frederick clearly has the edge in that department.'

Georgina said, 'Rose thinks a temporary butler would be best.'

'Yes, well I've spoken to Virginia on the telephone,' her uncle said. 'She favours Edward, and of the two of them so do you, don't you, my dear?'

She nodded. He said, 'Sorry, James. You're outvoted.'

'I always am. But what's wrong with Frederick? He's got spirit. He's a young man who knows where he's going. Edward's a nice fellow, but soft where it matters. Not his fault. The war's probably to blame for that. But he did go off to make his way in the world, and failed.'

'That wasn't his fault,' Georgina objected. 'Thousands of people . . .'

'All right, maybe that was harsh. But what about Daisy? From what I've seen, she's the drive behind Edward. Do we really want a butler who sits in the housemaid's pocket?'

'Daisy isn't like that. Don't be silly.'

'Well, from what Frederick says . . .'

Richard intervened. 'Look, we can put Edward above Frederick after Edward's performance the other night. I'll discuss it with Hudson. Unless he has any strong objections we must give the boy a chance.'

Hudson had no strong objections, though the very discussion of a candidate to stand in for him proved painful when Lord Bellamy raised it the next day. At least he had been able to diminish the ordeal by bringing with him to Hudson's bedside the reply from Mr and Mrs Trantor, just received, to say how delighted they would be to care for their old friend for as long as might be necessary. Dr Foley had been consulted by telephone and had confirmed that, subject to a final examination later that day, Hudson could be permitted to make the journey within twenty-four hours.

'We'll arrange for an ambulance to take you down, of course,' Lord Bellamy said. 'I'm sure Rose or Mrs Bridges will do your packing for you.'

'I'm very grateful for all the trouble you've taken, my lord.'

Hudson was sitting up, looking more relaxed and cheerful.

'The least we could do, after all you've done for us. You've carried a great deal of responsibility. I don't know what we shall do without you these next months . . .'

Richard realised he should not have said that. He went on hastily, '. . . but you mustn't rush things. Take as long as you like.'

'There's just the matter of my successor, my lord. I am sure that, as you suggest, Edward can manage. However, if you feel, for the benefit of the household, that it would be desirable to appoint a new butler – a permanent man – then I have no wish to be a burden . . .'

'There's no question of that. This post is yours, as long as you want it. When the time does come for you to retire, you'll be the best judge. Now, is that understood, once for all?'

Hudson nodded and replied huskily, 'I'm very grateful to your lordship.'

Then, left alone, he lay back and actually began to look forward a little to a break in the country, telling himself that it would, in fact, be no time at all before he was back in harness.

The following lunchtime Edward stood before him. They were alone in the pantry, the young man nervously at attention, the older seated in a wheelchair, with rugs about his legs. Two large, packed suitcases stood nearby.

'The keys to the silver cupboard,' Hudson intoned solemnly, handing them over. 'The keys to the cellar. The cellar book. Remember to record every single bottle that's drunk. And those are the household accounts. Reckon them up once a week, on Saturday mornings. And never drop behind with settling the bills. This house has a most valued reputation with the local tradesfolk.'

'Yes, Mr Hudson.'

'Lastly, here's my pantry book of useful advice I've recorded over the years, privately, for whoever should need it some day. You may borrow it, for the time being.'

Edward took the scrapbook reverentially.

'Remember,' Hudson was concluding, 'to be butler in this household is a sacred trust. Absolute loyalty and devotion to duty are what is asked of you.'

There was a knock at the door. Frederick was admitted, to announce that the ambulance was at the door. He gave Edward an old-fashioned look as he took up the suitcases and went out. Rose entered to push Mr Hudson out in his chair.

'Remember, Edward,' he said at the door, 'if there's ever any advice you need, don't hesitate to write to me, care of Mr and Mrs Trantor, the Post Office, Southwold.'

'Thank you, Mr Hudson.'

'Off we go, then, Rose.'

He held out his hand to Edward.

'Good luck, my boy.'

Edward watched him go. Then, left alone, turned around to survey his new surroundings with awe.

When the ambulance had gone, they all settled down to cold luncheon at the long table in the servants' hall. For a moment, Edward hovered beside Mr Hudson's accustomed place, uncertain whether to put out his hand for the chair. He caught Mrs Bridges' eye. An almost imperceptible shake of her head made him move along to his own usual seat.

There was an uncomfortable silence, in which no one moved. He felt Daisy nudge him.

'What?' he said aloud.

Frederick grinned.

Rose stepped into the breach: 'For what we are about to receive . . .'

CHAPTER THREE

A strange air of depletion hung over No. 165 Eaton Place.

The continued absence of Mr Hudson, by now well on the mend but facing a lengthy recuperative period, was a major absence from the downstairs 'family'. Being Ascot week, Edward, too, was away, his permanent duty as chauffeur having to take precedence over his temporary one as butler at the order of James, who had wished to be driven to the house of friends near the racecourse and valeted there. James could perfectly well have gone by train, taking Frederick with him as valet. His friends would have transported him locally during his stay. But he had ordered Edward to go, as a little act of getting his own back on the man whose choice as stand-in butler he had opposed. His own favourite, Frederick, was thus left as sole male servant at Eaton Place.

His duties were minimal, however. Upstairs was even more depleted than down. Lord and Lady Bellamy were in Germany, attending an international function and residing in the splendour of a castle whose owner, possessor of the blood royal, had insisted that they would be waited on hand and foot by his own staff and need not bring personal servants.

It left only Miss Georgina Worsley to be cared for; and that beautiful and wilful young lady was preoccupied with exciting new plans.

From the morning-room she rang for Frederick and ordered cocktail ingredients to be fetched. When he had put the tray down on the sideboard she opened the cupboard door and surveyed the bottles of variegated shapes, sizes and colours.

'I think I'll make a Sidecar,' she pronounced.

'Yes, miss. That's two parts brandy, one part Cointreau, the juice of a quarter of a lemon, crushed ice, and shake it well.'

'Thank you, Frederick. Are you sure that'll be strong enough, though? Lady Dorothy likes her cocktails with a terrific kick in them.'

'I think you'll find that quite satisfactory, miss,' Frederick said, and excused himself to answer the front door. A moment later he was back to announce 'Lady Dorothy Hale, miss.'

'Sorry I'm late, darling,' gushed Lady Dorothy as she almost ran into the room. She was in her late twenties, petite, with cropped auburn hair and an intriguingly snub nose. Bit of all right, Fred thought, not failing to note that she had given him a lightning appraisal in return.

'Paul's not with me,' he heard her telling her hostess. 'He's coming on, though. He telephoned at the last minute to say he was delayed at the studios. Oh, cocktails! Marvellous!'

'Frederick's just been reminding me how to mix a Sidecar. Would you like one?'

'Yes, please.'

Georgina set confidently about the task, saying, 'Thank you, Frederick, I'll ring if we need any more ice.'

'Very good, miss.' He bowed and went.

'I say!' Lady Dolly murmured after he had closed the door. 'What a divine-looking young man!'

Georgina was surprised. 'Frederick? I suppose he is, rather. But tell me about Paul Marvin.'

'Well, he's said to be Rumanian, but you never quite know with these film people. He's distinctly oily and full of artificial charm. Frankly, I'm rather bored with him but I thought you ought to meet him. Flatter him for a week or two, at least till you see whether you can wangle a job in one of his films.'

Georgina popped cherries on sticks into both their glasses and they went over to the settee. Dolly sipped.

'Ooh, what a divine cocktail!' She sipped again. 'Heavenly.'

Georgina need have had no doubts about the strength of her mixture. 'Gosh!' she said, after tasting it. 'I'll be tight by the time Mr Mervin gets here.'

'Nonsense.'

'Anyway, supposing he doesn't think I'm pretty enough for the films?'

'Of course he will. It's great fun, darling. You get ten shillings a day, just to sit in front of the camera and look alluring. Patsy Cremorne did it a few weeks ago, out at Islington or somewhere in the wilds. They all had to be in bathing costumes round a pool with no water in it.'

'Sounds chilly.'

'Apparently the arc lamps kept them all warm. They have these very strong lamps everywhere. I say, where's your tall, dark, handsome cousin?'

'James? Staying down at Ascot.'

Dolly pouted excessively and drained her glass. 'What a bore. I was hoping he'd be here. I adore him. Didn't you know?'

Georgina was amused. 'You? Seriously?'

'Of course I do. But it isn't recipro . . . gosh! . . . recip . . . ro . . . cated. He doesn't adore me.'

They heard the front door bell.

'That'll be Paul.'

'Oh, dear!' Georgina said, getting up and walking about. 'I'm nervous now.'

'Well, don't be. Look poised and cool and disdainful. Like Gloria Swanson. Take your cocktail in one hand, cigarette holder in the other, and lower your eyelids and sort of . . . smoulder.'

Georgina giggled. 'I'll try. I've never smouldered before.'

She had just time to strike a half-hearted attitude which she imagined might be appropriate before Frederick showed Paul Marvin in.

Dolly's description, though sketchy, had been accurate, Georgina thought. Charm emanated from the dapper man as obviously as an expensive but ostentatious perfume. He was middle aged, his hair engagingly greying, a monocle screwed into one bright eye. His clothing was tasteful and beautifully cut. A fresh carnation adorned his lapel and there were uncreased spats over his brilliantly-shone shoes.

He advanced straight to Georgina and bowed over her hand, just brushing the back of it with his lips.

'Miss Worsley. How delightful! And my Lady Dolly!' He

seemed to notice her for the first time, but merely nodded in her direction before turning back to Georgina. 'I am so sorry if I'm a little late. My star ripped a Paquin dress into a thousand pieces and stood on the set in her chemise until they carried her screaming to her dressing-room and gave her smelling salts. So we shoot no more today.'

From behind him, Dolly gave Georgina a look which could only signify 'He's making it all up, to impress you.'

'How fascinating,' Georgina told him. 'I mean, how awful. Poor dress. Poor you.'

'Ah, we are used to such scenes in the film studios, Miss Worsley.'

She seated him and poured him a cocktail, replenishing Dolly's glass and topping up her own. It was established that he had expected her to call him Paul, since everyone else did, though she didn't in turn offer him the use of her christian name.

'What actually is the film you're making?' she asked.

'*Paris by Night*. I have Carl Brisson, Anny Ondra, Max Reiler and Zita Young. My director is Miles Mander, who is a master.'

'It all sounds very thrilling.'

'It will be a superb moving picture.'

Dolly, who had demolished most of her cocktail already, put down the glass over-carefully and began to fish around a trifle hazily for her bag and gloves.

'Georgina, darling, I've simply got to fly,' she said. From the way she stood up it seemed that any immediate flight would be of less than stable nature, but she appeared resolved. Georgina pressed the bell. Dolly explained, 'Dear Robert's taking me to the Cochran revue. I'll give you a ring in the morning. 'Bye, Paul.'

He half-rose, then subsided. Georgina followed her to the door.

'The footman will get you a taxi, Dolly, she said.

At the recollection of Frederick's Roman features, Dolly paused distinctly and said, 'Oh! That would be nice.'

Frederick appeared at the door, his usual impassive self.

'A taxi for Lady Dorothy, please,' Georgina said.

'Very good, miss.'

'Look, Georgina, you stay and talk to Paul. I'll get my coat and things and just go. Go on . . .' Dolly insisted; and Georgina obeyed, shutting herself in the morning-room with Paul, who had risen to greet her return.

Frederick held Dolly's coat for her.

'Won't take a minute to get a cab, m'lady,' he told her. 'Plenty past here – though I can ring the rank if you wish.'

'Never mind, Frederick,' she said. 'It *is* Frederick, isn't it?'

'That's right, m'lady.'

'Yes. I remember you from when I came to a fancy dress party here some time ago.'

'That's right, m'lady. I remember you.'

'You do?'

'You was dressed as a nymph, m'lady.'

'So I was. How clever of you to remember.'

'I noticed you special, m'lady.'

She studied him for a moment. His expression told her nothing. The dark eyes were inscrutable.

'I'll see you out and get you a taxi, m'lady,' he said, and touched her elbow ever so slightly as he ushered her to the door.

However much she was aware of the superficiality of Paul Marvin's charm – and she believed Dolly had been a good deal less than fair to him, no doubt because he had clearly lost interest in her – Georgina found herself chatting unreservedly with him. He fascinated her with tales of the romantic world of the film studios, amused her with his semi-scandalous anecdotes of the private lives of the stars, and flattered her in an acceptable way. She was sorry when, at half-past seven, he regretted that he must take his leave, to be in time for a dinner appointment with some moving picture financiers from the U.S.A. But by then the suggestion which she had half hoped for, yet half feared, had been made and hesitantly agreed to.

'Then, that's settled, my dear. I will have the studio people telephone you next week for a costume fitting.'

'Yes, I see,' Georgina said, beginning to thrill as the idea sank in. 'Oh, Paul, I've always longed to be in a film. Oh, you dear, kind man!'

She kissed him impulsively, to his pleased surprise. He took the opportunity of asking, 'Maybe we can lunch together one day soon, yes?'

'If you like,' she agreed readily. 'I'll ring for the footman.'

'Please don't trouble. My flat is quite close to Sloane Square, so I shall walk. My dear Miss Worsley, I am so pleased that we are to be associated. My compliments, please, to Lord and Lady Bellamy.'

He bowed elaborately and kissed her hand again, then confidently let himself out of the room and the house. Georgina swallowed the rest of her neglected cocktail, whirled round the room in a solo waltz, and finished up before a mirror, striking a dramatic pose, head held high and eyelids provocatively lowered.

A few evenings later, Rose, sitting alone in the servants' hall, looked up from her sewing as a man came in from the area entrance. It took her more than a second to recognize Frederick. He wore a brown teddy bear overcoat she had never seen on him before and was just taking off a wide-brimmed fedora hat, such as she had seen American film stars wearing on the screen.

'You still up?' he said, cheerfully and superflously.

She looked at the wall clock. It showed eleven.

'Just finishing off some sewing. Look at you! Nice coat.'

He took it off. 'Yeh.'

'Want some cocoa?'

'No, ta. Just smoke a cigarette before I turn in, if you don't object.'

'Course not.'

She noted that the cigarette came from a slim silver case and that its aroma, when he lit it, was strangely pungent.

'What's that?' she asked.

'Balkan Sobranie. Turkish.'

'Bit dear, aren't they?'

'A bit. I prefer 'em.'

'You come into money, or something?' He followed her pointed glance at his coat, draped over a chair.

'Me? No. I reckon to put my wages by for a rainy day. Got to have a new coat sometime.'

He smiled patronisingly at the puzzlement on her face and proffered the open cigarette case. Rose hesitated, then took one. She didn't exactly like the unaccustomed taste; but there was something expensively exotic about it that made it pleasing, just the same.

When James got back from Ascot and heard Georgina's excited outpouring of her news his reaction was deflating, if characteristic.

'The wretched man doesn't have to go to the fitting with you, hang it!'

'He's the producer, darling. He's got to be there to approve that it fits me.'

'Oh, I'll bet he does!'

'Look, James, Paul Marvin's a well-known film producer. He's not likely to throw me on a couch at a costumier's shop in the Strand at ten-thirty in the morning and ravish me.'

'You don't know film producers.'

'How many do you know? I know this one, and he's not like that. At least, I don't think he is. Anyway, I met him through Dolly.'

'Huh! Dolly Hale's friends are a rotten, third-rate lot. And I have heard a lot about film people. They're all greedy, immoral and unreliable. I strongly object to you getting mixed up with them.'

Her beautiful eyes flashed up at him.

'Well, I *am* mixed up with them. So that's it, isn't it?'

He was compelled to retreat to a secondary position.

'Well, if you must have this dago at your costume fitting, I suppose you must. But I beg you, Georgina, please don't be seen lunching with him at the Savoy afterwards.'

'I told you it's arranged. It's the least I can do to thank him for giving me a part in his film.'

James's fragile temper broke. 'Now you're really talking like a prostitute!'

'As I'm appearing in a film as one, I might as well get in some practice.'

'Oh, God!'

As always, she hated upsetting him, knowing that his rudeness stemmed from his own basic discontentment and from a genuine concern for her well-being. She swallowed her resentment and tried conciliation.

'Listen, Jumbo, if you're worried about my undressing in front of Paul – and I don't for a moment believe it'll be necessary – I'll ask Dolly to come as my chaperone. Paul won't like the implication, but at least he'll have me alone for lunch afterwards.'

Her fair compromise came too late. Muttering that he didn't care what she did, he strode out of the room, with his familiar, childish slam of the door. Georgina sighed and tried to return to the state of euphoria in which she had been luxuriating earlier. It wouldn't come, however. By the evening, she knew that she must make some gesture towards easing the atmosphere. She telephoned Dolly and made the request.

'*Me* chaperone *you*!' Dolly exclaimed above the strains of her gramophone's 'My Heart Stood Still'. 'But that's too absurd. Anyway, surely there'll be a costume fitter there.'

'I know. It's all so stupid, but . . .'

'Besides, I can't. I'm going shopping – with my new lover.'

'Oh.'

'Yes. Isn't it exciting? His name's Alberto. Terribly handsome, and, my dear, he dances divinely. Italian, of course. Of the House of Montespiore di Cologna. He's here with me now. As soon as he's dressed we're off to join a party at the Opera.'

'How lovely,' Georgina said, unenthusiastically.

Dolly babbled on. 'All my friends are going to be madly jealous. I shall take him everywhere with me. Well, must fly, darling. So sorry about tomorrow. 'Bye.'

'Alberto, darling!' Dolly called, when she had replaced the receiver.

'Yes?' he replied, fastening his white tie.

'That was Miss Worsley on the telephone.'

'Go on!'

'Not "go on", darling. You must say, "Ees not true, uh?" Try it.'

'Ees not true, uh?' Frederick responded, entering the room, an opera cloak over one arm.

'Perfect!' Dolly cried delightedly. 'Bene, bene, mi amore.' She moved into his arms to kiss him. 'Now we must go. We'll need to get a taxi.'

'I'll get one,' Fred said automatically.

'No you won't, *Alberto*. The porter will see to it. Now, come along, you lovely man, and be a credit to me.'

'Hullo, Fred,' Rose said next morning, approaching lunch-time. 'Done the silver?'

'Yep.'

She peered close. 'I'll have to buy you a new razor for Christmas. Good job Mr Hudson isn't here.'

He ran fingers over his chin. There was faint but distinct rasping sound.

'Shows, does it? Got up in a bit of a hurry.'

'Late getting in again, was you?'

'Must have been.'

'I've washed your silk scarf for you.'

'Oh, ta, Rose.'

'Got most of the lipstick off.'

'Lipstick?'

'And perfume. What her ladyship uses.'

'Lots of ladies use that.'

'Wealthy ladies, yes. Here, do you nip in her ladyship's room and pinch a bit to put on your scarf to cut a bit of a dash, eh?'

'Who with?'

'Go on! You're not spending your time off on your own, Frederick Norton, so don't give me that.'

'My private life is private, Rose, like Mr Hudson always says.'

She gave him a conspiratorial smile.

'Only teasing. We've always ribbed each other a bit in this house. You can't bc in service in a big house with a staff but what you know a bit about each other's private affairs.'

'I know,' he said, with a seriousness that surprised her. 'That's one good reason for getting out of service.'

'Oh? And what's another?'

'There's better things to do than clean silver all day long.'

'I thought you was quite contented here. Is it because they didn't make you butler?'

'Nope. Mr Hudson'll be coming back, anyway.'

Rose moved closer to him, examining hard his impassive face.

'You're tired out, that's your trouble,' she deduced. 'Can't stay out half the night and be up fresh in the morning to do your work.'

'I know.'

'Look, slip up to your room after lunchtime and have a good sleep until tea. It's your afternoon off.'

'Thanks, Rose, but I can't. Got to slip down to the doctor's about my headaches.'

'You've had a lot of them lately. They getting worse?'

'Just the same. Thought I ought to see him about them, though.'

'Yeh. Fred . . .'

'Mm?'

'Watch how you go.'

'Don't worry about me, Rose.'

In the morning-room at that moment Lady Prudence Fairfax was saying to James, as they sipped sherry, 'I must say, it's frightfully good of you, James, bothering with your ageing Auntie Prue instead of some dizzy young flapper.'

'Quite honestly, Prue,' he said, 'I don't seem to know many dizzy young things these days. They're all either tiresome or married.'

'Well, it'll be very flattering to visit a film studio with a handsome man to escort me. You know, I'm so looking forward to it. I've never seen them making a film.'

'Nor have I.'

'Helen and Archie Croft were taken on to the set in Hollywood last year. Apparently they watched John Gilbert and some heavily painted woman with a Spanish name doing a love scene in a gondola. They met him afterwards. They said he was charming but rather common.'

James gave a grimace of distaste.

'Does Georgina know we're going to be there?' Prue asked. He shook his head. 'Give her a surprise.'

Daisy entered to announce luncheon. James asked her with some surprise, 'Where's Frederick?'

'He's gone to the doctor's about his headaches, sir. He could only get an early appointment, so Edward said it would be all right, as it's his half-day.'

'I see. Edward knows we want the car for half-past two?'

'It's arranged, sir.'

'Thanks. Come along, then, Aunt Prue.'

'Come this way, please, Lady Prudence,' Paul Marvin said, two hours later. 'Please mind your step. There are so many cables to the lamps.'

Followed by James, she picked her way carefully across the narrow space between the brick walls of the converted Islington warehouse and the backs of the plywood and canvas setting, blank on this side, but, as they emerged on to the set, transformed on the other by paint and light into the gaudy semblance of a seedy Parisian nightclub. Instead of the aroma of garlic-laden cooking, there was an equally heady smell of oil paint, size, dust, wood, canvas and perfume, drawing out of the surroundings by the heat of the clustered lamps, brilliant on their tall stands.

A strangely mixed company of men and women moved, stood or sat there. Reading a newspaper at one of the tables was a heavily made-up man of avaricious and untrustworthy aspect whose costume and long apron proclaimed him to be a waiter. Also seated – and discussing, James could hear, the seemingly incongruous subject of the runners at a forthcoming English provincial race meeting – were what looked, from his build and blue trousers and blouse, to be meant to be a French bargee, and a woman of similar proportions, whose blouse and trappings left no mistake that she was portraying a 'madame'. Several of her 'girls' lounged about the place, exaggeratedly made-up for the cameras and displaying alarming lengths of leg through the splits in their skirts. Their male compatriots of the *demi monde*, striped-shirted and capped, chatted with them and again James heard the name of a race meeting mentioned: this time it was Ascot, in connection with certain criticisms of the refreshment arrangements in the Royal Enclosure. Georgina was not in view.

Not even bothering to eye the revealed charms of these shapely girls, there moved about a throng of men of varying ages, sizes and shapes, clad in honest British working overalls. They were doing things to the lights, adjusting furniture, measuring distances with tapes, climbing and descending ladders, and mostly talking simultaneously, though seemingly under some sort of direction from others of their kind. An earnest, plain girl with a clip pad bearing a thick wad of paper hurried backwards and forwards, observing details of the scene and noting them, enabling one scene to move into another with smooth continuity.

Behind a group of bored-looking musicians, equipped with an accordion and other instruments suited to the general conception of a French night club, stood the awe-inspiring camera, being inspected minutely by the man who must certainly be its operator. Nearby stood the tweed-jacketed all-powerful director, a chubby, cheerful man, gesticulating carefully as he made his wishes known to a younger, more anxious looking colleague who was no doubt his assistant.

'My dear!' Prue exclaimed to James, 'Isn't it wonderful? So realistic.'

Paul Marvin, who was attired as neatly as if he had been visiting, explained, 'They are now lighting the set, ready for rehearsal. I will find you a chair, then you can sit here and watch.' He waved to someone and a chair was passed over. Lady Prue sat, while James remained standing behind her.

Marvin continued, 'In a few moments we shall rehearse and then shoot the brawl scene. Some special girls will be at those tables – Miss Worsley among them. At first, people are dancing and making love, as the music plays. Suddenly, down those steps will come Gaston, the lover of one of the girls. But she is in the arms of another man. Gaston draws a knife. A woman screams. They will all stand up, tables will be overturned, and a fight will begin.'

He held up a knife. James said, 'I say, that sounds a bit dangerous. Can't someone get hurt?'

Marvin grinned and shook his head. 'See.' He plunged the knife into his own chest. Lady Prudence's hand flew to her throat as she saw the blade go in, but then she looked sheepish as she heard the artificial rasp and realised that it had retracted into the knife handle and was made only of hard rubber, anyway.

'Everything is unreal,' Paul Marvin said deprecatingly of his industry. 'Even those walls of stone are soft plaster. They can tear like paper if someone is careless. Ah, there is Miss Worsley now. If you wish to speak with her before we start . . .?'

'No, no,' James answered, looking round for Georgina. 'Don't tell her we're here. We'll just keep out of the way.'

'Thank you,' Marvin said. 'It is better she can concentrate on her work. She will not see you, with the bright lights on her face. So, you will please excuse me?'

He bowed and went off towards the camera. The assistant director had begun to call everyone to order. Most of the technicians were retreating into the shadows behind the lights, while the actors and actresses were assuming their allotted positions and attitudes of, respectively, menace and cynical seductiveness.

Both James and Prue, having identified Georgina, were staring at her as if she were a stranger, and not a very wholesome-looking one at that. Her gaudy clothing was similar to that of the other tarts in the scene, though, if anything, a shade more revealing. Her face was thickly powdered and painted and her hair done in a way she would never have worn it in Belgravia.

'Just as well Richard can't see her dressed like that,' Prue said.

Half impressed, half angry at the spectacle, James replied, 'She's got better legs than any of the rest of 'em.'

'Yes, hasn't she? Oh, it's all too fascinating.'

She fell silent and paid attention as the assistant director explained the action to the cast.

'Pay attention, girls. You'll have a tough guy each, seated at your table. The boys are just coming in from make-up. Now, when the director calls for action, you'll start to pet and cuddle with your partners. Make it good and passionate, O.K.? Then I'll clap my hands once and shout "Gaston". On that cue, I want you all to stop what you're doing, look up the steps over there, react to Gaston coming down, get up in a panic and overturn the tables as you do. All understood?'

There was a murmur of assent. The assistant director addressed himself to Georgina.

'Gaston comes down across the dance floor, moving like a panther straight up to your table, dear.'

'Mine?' echoed Georgina, clearly alarmed to be singled out on her first day.

'That's right, honey. He seizes hold of your partner, drags him on to the dance floor. They fight and Gaston gets knifed. O.K.?'

'W... what do you want me to do?'

'Just stand and look like you're screaming. Can you scream darling?'

'Actually scream? I suppose so.'

'Then it's better you do. Make it look more realistic. All of you, make like you're real scared. They say some day there'll be a way of recording actual sound on films – I don't think! But the more you scream and jabber, the more scared you'll look. Right, now, here come the boys.'

A group of Apaches entered the set, to be shepherded to

their respective positions by the assistant director. He took one of them by the arm and steered him to Georgina's table. The man was tall and dark, with gummed-on sidechops and a smouldering cigarette in the corner of his mouth.

He was also Frederick.

Georgina's astonishment on recognising him was more than matched by his stare of horror when he saw her. Watching from behind the scenery, at a point from which she had not spotted James Bellamy and Lady Prue, nor had been seen by them, Lady Dorothy Hale nudged the girl-friend she had brought to watch and giggled softly, 'That's it! Do look at their faces. Oh, Freddy'll kill me – or she will.'

Fred and Georgina were still staring at one another, transfixed. The assistant director's whistle blew and he shouted to everyone to stand by for rehearsal. Frederick looked round in panic.

'You two!' the assistant director shouted. 'We haven't got all day. Take the girl on your lap.'

Georgina told Frederick in a low voice, 'Come on. We'll have to.'

'Yes, miss,' he responded miserably, and moved to obey.

No sooner had they adopted the position than another voice rang out which alarmed them twice as much. It was unmistakably James Bellamy's.

'Stop! Just a minute!'

'Oh my God!' Dolly Hale gasped to her companion. 'It's James Bellamy. That's done it.'

James had stepped out on to the set. He was raging.

'What the hell is this man doing here? Who engaged him?'

Prue moved forward to try to restrain him, urging him not to make a scene. He ignored her.

'This man's my servant. He's no right to be here. Who's responsible for this? Where's Marvin?'

Hazarding everything, Dolly Hale ran on to the set to face James.

'James, please,' she begged. 'It was only a joke. I arranged it for a bit of fun. If I'd known you were going to be here . . .'

The stunned silence of actors and technicians had broken now into a confusion of chatter and growls of complaint. From far behind the camera Paul Marvin was hurrying forward as well as the writhing cables and other obstacles would allow.

'I might have known you'd be behind it,' James snarled at Dolly. He seized Georgina by the hand and tried to drag her off the set, shouting at Frederick, 'And you get back to Eaton Place at once, and wait in for me. That's an order, Norton.'

Frederick was bold enough to point out, reasonably, 'But I've been engaged for an afternoon's work, sir. It's my afternoon off, and it's not my fault.'

'I don't care what you've been engaged for. Get out of that ridiculous costume and go home at once, d'you hear?'

Georgina released herself from James's grip.

'You can't do that to him, James,' she protested, as Paul Marvin reached them, clearly bewildered.

'Yes I can. You go and change, too, Georgina.'

'I'll do nothing of the sort.'

'James,' Dolly Hale pleaded, 'you can't upset everything like this. They're making a film.'

'What is going on?' Paul Marvin managed to ask at last. James turned on him.

'It's this woman's fault. I've never heard of anything so infantile and irresponsible in my life.'

Marvin called loudly, 'Clear the set. Save the lights.' The bright colours faded abruptly from the surroundings as the lamps were switched off, making everything suddenly dark and oppressive as the actors straggled away, lighting cigarettes and casting curious glances at the figures at the centre of this unrehearsed drama: the tall, angry gentleman and the well dressed lady anxious beside him; the younger woman looking desperately at the made-up actor, who was glaring daggers at her; the tarted-up actress pouting crossly; and the troubled producer, his habitual suavity lost.

'Georgina,' James said, 'are you coming back with Prudence and me in the car, or not?'

'No, I am not,' she said in a firm voice. 'I am staying here to do my job. Now, go away. You've no business to be here.'

James stared at her, but she stood defiantly. Paul Marvin asked, 'What is all the difficulty, please?'

Frederick answered him. 'I'm sorry, Mr Marvin, but it's all over me. I'm Major Bellamy's servant. I didn't know nothing about Miss Georgina being here. I'd best go home now, if you can get somebody in my place.'

He turned to Georgina. 'Excuse me, miss. Honest, I didn't know.'

'I know it isn't your fault, Frederick.'

'No, it's all mine,' Dolly Hale insisted. 'I'm sorry, Georgina, darling. It was only a joke, though.'

'Well, it wasn't a very amusing one. I don't like to see servants embarrassed, ever.'

'Oh, Freddy wouldn't have minded. It's only because James had to come and spoil everything. We're old friends, Freddy and I.'

'Are you? Well, you're no friend of mine any more, Dolly Hale. Just leave me, please. I've got work to do.'

Sensing an end to the disturbance, the hovering assistant director called out, 'O.K. everyone. Stand by again for rehearsal, please.'

But Paul Marvin said quietly to Georgina, 'I'm sorry, my dear, but since I do not wish to upset Lord Bellamy's family I wish you to get changed. I shall come and speak with you later. Please . . .'

Georgina hesitated for a moment. Then, with a last resentful glare at James, she stalked away.

The assistant director's whistle blew, the lights came up; and the illusion was recreated.

'Hullo, Fred,' Rose greeted him with surprise. 'You back already? Had any tea?'

'Yep.'

'There's some left in the pot if you fancy another cup,' Mrs Bridges said.

'No thanks.'

Daisy asked, 'What did the doctor say?'

'Eh?'

'About your headaches. Rose told us . . .'

'Oh, that. Gave me some medicine. The Major in yet?'

'Yes. Proper mad about something, Eddie said. Him and Lady Prudence came out of them studios nearly as soon as they'd gone in, and him looking like thunder. Told Eddie to drive back here at once.'

'That all?'

'Eddie doesn't listen in, you know that. Why you asking, anyway?'

The morning-room bell interrupted the conversation.

'I'll go, if that's Lady Prudence leaving,' Frederick said. 'I want to see the Major.'

'In your off-duty suit?'

'He won't mind, this once.'

He went up, to find that her ladyship had, after all, been seen out personally by the Major. The latter motioned him into the morning-room. Frederick stood to attention.

'Frederick, I wasn't going to speak to you about this afternoon's performance until tomorrow. Since you're here, I think we'd better discuss it now.'

'Yes, sir.'

'I'm all for an occasional joke, but I don't think, in all fairness, you can expect me to turn a blind eye to this one.'

'Beg pardon, sir, but I didn't know about it.'

'Knowing Lady Dorothy Hale, I'm prepared to believe you. I hope, otherwise, you'd have come and warned me and I'd have put a stop to it. I brought you in and gave you a good job after the war, because you'd been my servant and I trusted you.'

'I'm very grateful to you, sir.'

'Right. Then that's all . . .'

'If I might interrupt, sir.'

'What?'

'Just to explain, sir. You see, sir, I'm very grateful to you, and to his lordship and her ladyship. I have been happy in service here, sir. Only, lately, I've been a bit unsettled.'

'Oh, that business about Edward's promotion. I understand that.'

'Not only on that account, sir.' Frederick swallowed, continuing to stare straight ahead of him. 'You see, since Lady Dorothy called round here when you were away for Ascot, and then asked me to join her and some of her friends for dinner at a café . . .'

'She *what?*'

'. . . I've had the opportunity of seeing how other people live. She's been very good to me, and I've found I can, like, make my own way with people – Lady Dolly's sort of people, sir.'

'Oh, you can, can you?'

'I'm a bit ambitious, as you know, sir. So I've decided to give up service and take my chance in the outside world, if you'd be good enough to accept my notice, sir.'

James moved slightly, compelling Frederick's gaze to meet his.

'Are you telling me that Lady Dolly's been taking you about London with her?'

'Yes, sir. She's been very kind, buying me clothes and nice things . . .'

'Have you no pride, man? Has she been paying you money to go around with her? Actual cash?'

'She gave me some money last week, sir.'

'God! You, Trooper Norton of His Majesty's Life Guards, my old soldier servant and footman – little better than a kept man, a gigolo! Are you mad?'

'I've nothing to be ashamed of, sir.'

'Well, you jolly well should have.'

'Can I take it that you accept my notice, then?' Frederick asked, unshaken.

'What the hell else can I do?'

'Thank you, sir.'

He left the room with dignity and returned to the servants' hall. Mrs Bridges was in her armchair, sewing. Edward, who had just come in from the garage, was leafing through a magazine, with Daisy peering at it over his shoulder. Rose was darning. Fred sat down at the table.

'Well,' he said, looking over them all almost contemptuously. 'Time to say cheerio.'

' "Cheerio"?' Mrs Bridges asked, glancing up without genuine curiosity.

'That's right. I'm leaving.'

All their heads were up now.

'You . . . got the push?' Edward asked.

'Give meself the push. That's what.'

'Got a better job, eh?'

Frederick caught Rose's eye. She was watching him with knowing cynicism.

'I think I can guess, Fred, can't I?' she asked.

'Can you?'

'You've got a wealthy lady friend who wants to marry you.'

Their gazes remained locked, ignoring the others, oblivious of their audible reactions.

'Not getting married, Rose. I've been seeing quite a bit lately of Lady Dolly Hale. Seeing all of her, if you really want to know.'

'So that's who it was! All that expensive perfume on your scarf. Been on intimate social terms, haven't you?'

'The Major knows all about it. I told him.'

Mrs Bridges burst in, 'It's disgusting, Frederick. I've heard of ladies of title amusing themselves being friendly with a footman when it's suited them. But just you remember, that Lady Dolly's a madcap and gets herself into the papers over men.'

'I can get on with people of her sort,' Frederick answered coolly. 'I can make a good living on the films and escorting and dancing with ladies at tea-dance places. I know I can, because they all said I can. Only the other night, at the opera . . .'

'Ho! So we go to the opera now, do we? The royal box, I suppose.'

'No, the one next to it. Anyway, Lady Dolly told me I was wasted as a servant. "With your looks and your sex appeal," she said, "you could conquer London." '

'I don't call that conquering London, any more than a tom-cat out on the wall in the moonlight.'

'Mrs Bridges!' Rose protested, more shocked by this than by Frederick's revelations.

'What a thing to say in front of my wife!' Edward agreed, less than seriously.

Mrs Bridges shook her head. 'Time she learnt a thing or two about life – especially if she's going on working in *this* house. All I can say is thank the Lord Mr Hudson isn't here. If he knew his footman was carrying on with a lady what's a friend of the family, I think he'd drop dead.'

Frederick got up, grinning, and went to the door, pausing there to say, 'One day when I'm a famous film star out in Hollywood I'll send you all my photo, autographed, so you can show it to your pals and say "That's Frederick Norton, as used to work here as footman. Done well for himself, hasn't he?" Cheerio.'

He went out, leaving them in varying degrees of devastation. Out from their lives forever went ex-Trooper Frederick Norton. And for all her expression of relief that he hadn't been present to hear such scandal, Mrs Bridges secretly prayed that it might not be long before Angus Hudson might return. Nothing – nothing at all – seemed any longer to be like it had been in the good old days before that horrid war.

CHAPTER FOUR

By nearly the middle of that year, 1927, Mr Hudson was back at his post, fit to resume all his duties. Edward was as pleased as anyone to find him so well, though perhaps he had unconsciously fancied that there might be some small portion of the butler's capacity left for him. It was anti-climatic to step down to mere chauffeur/valet again and, since no replacement had been hired for the errant Frederick, he found himself doing footman's work as well. A modest increase in his wages helped to compensate him for both extra duties and loss of his temporary status.

Parliament had just gone into recess. Virginia was away in Paris with William and Alice, the latter on the verge of coming-out into society and thus being indulged in a visit to the Collections to choose the appropriate clothes. Rose had gone with them.

By a convenient chance, Richard's friend Lord Berkhamstead had recently offered him the use at any time of his fishing lodge in the Scottish Highlands, a place Berkhamstead seldom used himself. Feeling the strain towards the end of a busy session, Richard suddenly decided to take up the offer. James and Georgina were to accompany him, all travelling up in the car, driven by Edward, while Hudson, Mrs Bridges, Daisy and Ruby would go by train.

'I don't think I want to go to Scotland,' Georgina pouted when told of the plan. 'It'll rain all the time.'

'Of course, you don't have to come, my dear,' Richard told her. 'I just think it would be a pity not to. Carnochie's a wonderful place. Plenty of good fresh air will do you a world of good.'

'No traffic, no noise,' James urged her. 'A chance to tramp over the heather, fish for salmon . . .'

'I can't fish.'

'I'll teach you.'

'How far will the nearest cinema be?'

Richard smiled. 'Seventy miles – over a rough road.'

'Oh, lord!'

'Take a good book to read, then,' James said. 'Anyway, you've got to come. We're closing this house up.'

'Oh, very well. But don't blame me if I'm sick in the car, travelling all that way.'

None of the servants, except, of course, Mr Hudson, had ever visited Scotland. He smiled indulgently in the train as he listened to excited chatter about kilts and bagpipes and caber-tossing and all the rest of their exaggerated fancies. But as the Highland scenery began to appear outside the windows he felt excitement of his own stirring and didn't hesitate to draw their attention to the privilege they had been granted visiting this 'paradise on earth'.

There proved to be nothing paradisial about the prettily situated lodge once the kitchen door had been opened and the state of the interior witnessed. It was a largish room, full of angles and obstacles, and it needed only one glance from Mr Hudson and the pop-eyed Mrs Bridges at his elbow to tell that it was as dirty as it was disorderly. Acrid smoke hung on the air, emitted by a dingy black coal-fired range, at which a fair-haired woman in a dark blue dress stooped and fretted.

'Good day, Mrs . . . ?' Hudson greeted her tentatively. She turned and regarded him without reply. Her face was thin and somewhat lined, though Hudson doubted that she was beyond her thirties.

He continued, 'You are expecting us, I think? Lord Bellamy's party.'

At last she stood up, unsmiling and without any expression of greeting, let alone deference.

'The landlord's letter arrived by mail-boat only this morning,' she said, in the lilting Highland accent. 'McKay and myself had no warning of you.'

Mrs Bridges had pushed forward and was staring at the

range in disbelief and disgust. Smoke oozed from every one of its crevices.

'I hope I'm not expected to cook their dinner on that!' she exclaimed.

'This is Mrs Bridges, our cook,' Hudson explained. 'It's Mrs McKay, I believe?' In the continued absence of any welcoming response he said hastily, 'Well, I'll leave you ladies to the kitchen arrangements. Excuse me.' He withdrew thankfully, only to run into a frowning Daisy, emerging from what was evidently the parlour.

'Mr Hudson, it ain't half damp in here. And the grate's full of soot.' He sighed, and explained the position. A shriek from the kitchen sent them both hurrying there. Ruby, still wearing her hat and coat, stood with her hands over her mouth at the larder door she had opened.

'A dead bird!' she was repeating.

Hudson looked in and grimaced. 'A wee grouse. Last year's, by the smell of it.'

Mrs McKay said tonelessly, 'The larder has not been touched since last season's shooting party left. Give it to me and I will burn it.'

Hudson obliged, then turned to his staff.

'There, now, we must all get our coats off, roll up our sleeves, and set to work. His lordship, the Major and Miss Georgina will be here shortly. The place must be made as clean and comfortable as possible before they arrive. Really, all this smoke! Daisy, switch the light on, if you please.'

Daisy obediently went to the switch. Nothing happened when she pressed it. Hudson turned to Mrs McKay.

'Is the electricity not connected, Mrs McKay?'

'The generator is broken down. You'll have to be using oil lamps for the time being.'

Hudson and Mrs Bridges exchanged glances. Then a shout from the now-recovered Ruby told them that the luggage brake had arrived, and all became preoccupying bustle.

'Well!' declared Mrs Bridges later, as she surveyed the left-over remains of the tinned tomato soup, tinned ham and tinned peaches which Hudson had served in the dank sitting-room, the dining-room having proved utterly impossible to use. 'Well! I hope I never have to serve up a luncheon like that again as long as I live. I hope you explained that I'd ordered ahead for the groceries but they haven't arrived.'

'Of course, Mrs Bridges,' Hudson reassured her for the third time. 'His lordship quite understood. It was lucky there was that bottle of champagne left over from their picnic basket. There was only whisky to offer them before luncheon, and Miss Georgina dislikes it. The poor girl looks thoroughly miserable, huddled by that fire. I explained that the wood box is empty and that it takes peat a long time to burn up.'

'Get those scraps out of my sight, Ruby,' Mrs Bridges ordered. 'Then we'll all get on cleaning up this pigsty. If I'm to work in here for ten days I'm not having it in this state.'

Hudson tried to placate her. 'Never mind, Mrs Bridges. From tomorrow we shall be serving them, and ourselves, with some good fresh trout from the sea loch and salmon from the river.'

'Not out of these pots, we won't. Come along, Daisy. You lend a hand, too.'

The door suddenly opened, without a knock, and a man entered. He closed the door behind him and stood surveying them disdainfully. He was tall and straight-backed, with craggy features, permanently tanned by sun, wind and rain; the features of a man of the outdoors.

'You will be Lord Bellamy's household, no doubt,' he said, as though it were an accusation.

Mr Hudson stepped forward to confront him.

'That is correct. And who might you be?'

'I am Roderick McKay, head ghillie to Lord Berkhamstead.'

'Good evening to you.'

'We were not informed of your visit in time. Nothing is ready. You'll be wise to pack your trunks and return to London.'

'I'm sorry, but I don't think Lord Bellamy is considering any such thing.'

'It will not be comfortable here. You can go and tell his lordship that from me.'

'I certainly will not.'

As the edge of Mr Hudson's voice sharpened, Mrs Bridges quickly said to Ruby, 'Ruby, go and get your room ready.'

'Oh, Mrs Bridges,' the girl replied, 'not by myself. This house gives me the creeps.'

McKay looked at her, then said. 'The lass is right. This old lodge has seen some history, I can tell you. The first Laird of Carnochie fought at the Battle of Culloden, in the last stand of the Highlanders against the Hanoverian King George. That was a tragic day for Scotland. The Laird himself was greviously wounded. They say his servant and his piper lifted him, bleeding from a severed arm, onto a crofter's handcart and wheeled him over the mountain yonder to this very house, to escape from the men of Butcher Cumberland. They hid him in a loft, but he died of his wounds and they took him and buried him secretly at dead of night, to a piper's lament at some spot nearby on the hill, deep in the heather. But to this very day no one knows where.'

McKay's gaze shifted directly to Ruby's eyes.

'The only thing certain is that the Laird of Carnochie returns here from time to time of a dark night, for those who can hear him, groaning with the pain of his terrible wounds as he lies pale and bleeding on the handcart that carried him here from the field of Culloden. God rest his soul.'

A silence hung for long moments as McKay continued to stare implacably at the petrified Ruby, while the others looked on registering varying degrees of trepidation and concern. A sudden rumble of what might have been thunder or gunfire brought little shrieks from both Ruby and Daisy. Edward had to swallow hard before he could ask, 'What's that?', thoroughly expecting to be told that it was the Battle of Culloden still spiritually raging.

McKay answered, 'Did you not pump up the water?'

'Water?'

The ghillie indicated an old-fashioned hand-pump under the kitchen sink. 'It needs to be pumped up night and morning, and in between if anyone takes a bath. Has Mrs McKay not told you? That rumbling is the tank running nearly empty. If it does, with the stove lit, you will be having a real explosion.'

'Edward!' Mr Hudson ordered urgently. 'The pump will be your responsibility. Look lively, now, before the tank runs dry.'

Edward leaped willingly to obey, as the women moved instinctively further away from the range. Mr Hudson said to the ghillie. 'If you will kindly wait a moment, Mr McKay, I will ascertain whether his lordship wishes to see you.'

The man stood there, impassive and rock-like. He had not shifted his position by the time Hudson returned.

'His lordship is up resting in his bedroom, but his son, Major James Bellamy, wishes to have a word with you in the sitting-room.'

He led the still silent McKay away. Over the clank of the pump and Edward's gasps of effort, the three women heard a wind rising, quickly followed by sharp flurries of rain against the window-panes.

'Fat lot we're going to see of the blinking Highlands of Scotland at this rate,' Daisy grumbled. 'Might just as well have stopped in London, if you ask me.'

'I wish we had,' Ruby wailed. 'I don't like it here. I don't like it at all.'

Mrs Bridges gave her usual snort of impatience at Ruby's helplessness; but she had to admit to herself that she wasn't enamoured of Carnochie, either.

'It's McKay, isn't it?' James asked pleasantly, when Hudson had shown in the ghillie and retired.

'It is.'

'This weather going to pick up?'

'It might – and then it might not. There is little telling in these parts.'

'Mmm. Well, never mind the weather. I wanted a word with you about the fishing.'

'The fishing?'

'Yes. I'd like to go out and try for a salmon as soon as I can.'

'You'll be wasting your time, sir. Did not Lord Berkhamstead warn you that ours is a late river?'

'He certainly didn't. He told my father there'd be plenty of fishing.'

The ghillie gave a slight, pitying sigh. 'His lordship is so seldom here. I am afraid Lord Bellamy has been misinformed. It will not be worth your while to unpack a rod.'

'But that's absurd . . . .!'

The ghillie shook his head. 'There will be no fish in the river now.'

James struck the arm of his chair. 'Dammit, we've come all the way from London to fish for salmon, and you say there are no fish! We can't shoot yet and we don't stalk. So what the hell is there to do in this place?'

'There are good walks and fine scenery.'

James's answer to that was to glance towards the window, against which the wind-whipped rain was now positively lashing. McKay's face, angular-shadowed in the gloom, showed neither sympathy nor concern.

When James got rid of the visitor he went looking for his father. Meeting Hudson on the way, he paused to tell him the unwelcome news. The butler's eyebrows rose high when he heard it and he seemed about to say something, but merely came out with, 'Very disappointing, sir. We must hope for the weather to clear up, at least.'

Then Georgina came down, and James told her, with more petulance than he had used in speaking to Hudson. To his annoyance, she had no sympathy to give him. In fact, after a display of 'I told you so!' on first viewing the place in which they were to spend the next ten days, Georgina suddenly seemed to relax and become absorbed in a book she picked out from amongst the few the lodge could offer. Irritably, James asked what it was that seemed to have made her oblivious to discomfort within and vile weather without. She showed him the title on the volume's spine: *Clearances in the Scottish Highlands.*

'It's about the aftermath of the '45,' she told him. 'Jumbo, we treated them abominably. The English landlords drove thousands of simple Highland crofters off their land, just because they wanted room to graze their sheep. I suppose that's how Berkhamstead's family got this place; and look at it – being left to rot away, almost.'

James scowled. 'Your book's probably prejudiced. I bet it was written by a Scot. They're always going on about the wicked English. No wonder they're so dour and rude and gloomy, like that man McKay.'

'Well, I don't wonder he's put out. All this time with the place empty, then suddenly a crowd of people arrive with only a few hours' warning.'

Hudson came in at that moment with tea things.

'You see,' James said to Georgina. 'Tea bang on time. Some people can manage well enough under difficulties.'

Hudson permitted himself a little self-satisfied smirk on behalf of the staff. He asked Georgina, 'Shall I serve it now, miss, and not wait for his lordship?'

'Better leave him, if he's still asleep,' James answered, overlooking the fact that only a few minutes earlier he had been about to go up and pour out upon his father his own grievance.

Hudson poured tea and milk. James asked him, 'Hudson, what d'you make of that fellow, McKay? Curious chap, eh?'

'McKay is the head ghillie here, sir. Born and bred in these parts I imagine.' He paused before answering the unasked part of the question. 'I would not seek to question his knowledge of the local river, sir.' He handed them their cups and saucers.

'Mmm. Thanks, Hudson, that'll be all.'

'Thank you, sir, miss.' The butler withdrew.

The fire had begun to perk up a little and the tangy smell of the smouldering peat was permeating the air. The light in the room was fading quickly under the shadow of the lowering clouds. It would soon be quite dark.

James sipped his tea and sat back, cradling the saucer on his lap.

'This place is quite romantic, don't you think?' he asked uncharacteristically. Georgina was surprised, but she nodded warm agreement.

'Oh, yes. I feel very . . . different here, already. So quiet and dreamy and . . . and the air's so fresh and cool.'

'It's the sort of place where people . . . fall in love.'

'Oh, yes. Definitely.'

'Or suddenly realise how much in love they are – having not had time to think about these things.'

She was staring into the fire, not really listening to his words any more; simply entranced by the atmosphere of the surroundings.

'Yes,' she said almost dreamily. 'I could easily fall in love in the Highlands.'

The reverie lasted for long seconds before James spoke again.

'Georgina . . .'

'Mm?'

'Is it . . . really too late? For us? We . . . neither of us . . . seem to have anyone special in view, do we? So . . .'

She turned the big, luminous eyes towards his anxious face.

'Please don't, James. You'll spoil everything.'

'But you do love me. I *know* you do.'

'Of course I love you, darling. Only . . .'

The door opened and Richard came bustling in. His eyes lit up when he saw the tea tray.

'Oh, capital! I wondered whether we'd get any. I say, I must have been more tired than I thought I was. I slept like a child.'

Georgina poured for him.

'You need a good rest, Uncle Richard. No politics, no speeches . . .'

'No fish,' James would have put in, in his normal mood; but at the moment there was no acid in him. He said nothing. He was watching Georgina as he listened to his father saying to her, 'It's so relaxing here, I wonder anything ever gets done – if it does. I daresay nobody plots or shouts or schemes. They just get on with their honest, simple lives. We Londoners could learn from these people. How not to be in a hurry, and how to enjoy life while we can.'

Richard sat down with them. The little clatter of their cups on their saucers, the hiss of the fire and the buffeting of the wind and rain were the only sounds as they sat there, two of them in reverie, the other's suddenly-aroused thoughts awhirl.

The whole household slept well that night, apart for its humblest member – Ruby. Lying in the iron bed, beneath the disquieting shape of an antlered head affixed to the wall, she woke suddenly from what had been a good sleep into alarmed awareness. What she heard as she lay there sent her thinking of flying out of bed and out of her room, to burst in frantically on Mrs Bridges. It was more the fear of what might happen to her if she were to leave the comparative security of her bed than the scolding she knew she would get from Mrs Bridges that made her stay where she was; but she pulled up the sheet to cover her whole head.

She had heard the crunching of the wheels of the handcart on which the mortally wounded Laird was being brought home from Culloden.

Next morning she braved wrath by telling her tale.

'Couldn't Daisy sleep in my room tonight, Mrs Bridges?' she pleaded.

'No she could not,' was the indignant reply. 'Whatever next!'

But while Mrs Bridges had reacted to Ruby's story with scorn, and Edward with mockery, Mr Hudson, who had listened seriously, said nothing, but went about his duties with a thoughtful air.

The weather had let up, outbreaks of quite warm sun alternating with cooling cloud. The air almost effervesced and everyone's spirits – excepting again Ruby's – were correspondingly higher. Mrs McKay, who lived with her husband in a cottage nearby, was as dour as ever, but not hostile and she worked as hard as any of them to improve the kitchen. Questioned again about the electricity generator, she replied vaguely that she believed some spare part was needed and had been ordered. There was no knowing when it might turn up.

Mr Hudson made a note to get Edward to have a look at the generator. He might just be able to make a temporary repair. But Edward was away for the day, driving his lordship over to the home of a political friend who lived forty miles away. They would not be back until evening.

Richard had invited James and Georgina to drive over with him. Both had declined. Georgina was enjoying the lassitude of simply sitting about and reading her absorbing book, with the occasional short stroll along the heather-banked pathways which criss-crossed Lord Berkhamstead's estate. James took every opportunity to accompany her, slipping his arm through hers and wondering at the new radiance of her skin and eyes. His mind raced ahead as he tried to decide what next to say to her, but daytime and the fresh air seemed inappropriate to his feelings, and they talked only commonplaces.

After lunch, Mr Hudson announced that he, too, would be taking a stroll. He was going down into the little port of Camochie itself to have a look around. He invited Mrs Bridges to go with him, but she was yawning post-prandially and replied that with 'such air' she would just have to get down for forty winks.

Wearing his coat and bowler hat, Hudson made an incongrously formal figure amongst the villagers and the fisherfolk. The irony did not occur to him that he, of all the Bellamy household, should have been the one to have blended most easily into what was almost his native heath. But he had been long away, and, for all the remnants of his accent and beliefs, he was a Londoner by habit and appearance, if not completely at heart. He found himself observing the locals as if he were in a foreign land.

Perhaps this objectivity was responsible for his chancing to notice something which he might otherwise have missed. He was leaning on a rail close to the small jetty, enjoying the strong sea smell, the dance of the sunlight on the water, the soaring and swooping of the gulls. A dinghy bobbed at the foot of some sea-lapped stone steps near him. Two burly, blue-jerseyed men in it were receiving heavy fish-boxes, being passed down to them by another man, who was taking them from a handcart.

When the last box was aboard, the men in the dinghy cast

off and rowed laboriously the short distance out to a fishing-boat at moorings. Lingering on idly, enjoying this agreeable break from duty, Mr Hudson watched the boxes being passed up out of the dinghy to men on the fishing-boat. As soon as the operation had been completed and the dinghy had turned back towards the jetty, the fishing-boat cast off and turned her prow towards the distant shape of Skye.

A clock chimed, causing Mr Hudson to look at his watch. He began to walk hurriedly away. A sudden thought halted him in his tracks, and he turned to look first at the receding boat, then at the returned dinghy, and finally at the empty handcart.

His mind was ablaze with inspiration as he strode back to the lodge.

Edward arrived back in time for late supper. He sniffed eagerly at the delicious smell of kippers frying in the lamplit kitchen. He kissed Daisy, then rubbed his hands together appreciatively.

'Nothing like a nice kipper, Mrs Bridges.'

'Huh! I don't know whether I'm frying kippers or old boots in this light. I just hope they get done right, that's all.'

'They look lovely,' said Daisy, peering into the sizzling pan. 'You know, I'm beginning to like it here, now we've got the hang of things.'

'It's all right for you, Daisy. You've got young eyes. Mr Hudson, can't we do nothing about that electric light?'

'Yes,' he agreed. 'Edward, as soon as we've finished supper I'd like you to take a lamp and come with me to the generator house. There might be something you can fix up.'

'Sure, Mr Hudson,' Edward agreed willingly. 'Hullo, Ruby. The old Laird of Carnochie been at you yet?'

'That will do, Edward,' Mr Hudson said sharply. 'We'll have none of your feeble jokes at Ruby's expense.'

'No, Mr Hudson. Sorry.'

Light or no light, Mrs Bridges' expert instinct had enabled her to cook the kippers to perfection. 'More luck than good judgment,' was all she would concede in answer to unanimous praise. 'I really can't go on managing with just lamps.'

'Come along, Edward,' Mr Hudson ordered, rolling his napkin. 'And Ruby – off away to your bed. You looked washed out, girl.'

'Stick some cotton wool in your ears,' Edward couldn't restrain himself from adding. A look from Mr Hudson made him take up one of the oil lamps and lead the way out into the black night.

The stone hut which housed the generator was some thirty yards apart from the lodge. The interior smelt of oil and metal. They circled the machine, looking for the clasps that would enable the engine cover to be raised, and as they did so Mr Hudson raised his head and sniffed another smell.

'Just a moment, Edward. Bring the lamp through here, into this other room.'

It was at once cooler, and damp. 'Cor!' Edward exclaimed disgustedly. 'Fish!'

The aroma of wet fish, so less attractive than that of frying kippers, was undoubtedly of recent origin. Mr Hudson looked round with knowing eyes, taking in the marble slab with the single water-tap about it and buckets beneath. In a shadowy corner stood a stack of fish-boxes.

'Fishy is the word, Edward,' he said, and motioned his companion back to the generator room, where it soon became apparent that nothing Edward could contrive would get the machine going. They returned to the lodge and not long afterwards went to their bedrooms.

As she had expected and feared, Ruby heard the handcart again that night. Again, she buried her head under her sheets and muttered the only scraps of prayer she knew.

Mr Hudson, too, heard the cart, but did not pray. He had been waiting for the sound and had not undressed in anticipation of it. Swinging himself off the top of his bed and slipping on his shoes, he lit his lamp cautiously, keeping his body between it and the window so as to show no light, then took it up and went quietly downstairs. Slipping out by the kitchen door, he crept quietly towards the generator house. He could see light there, and movement, and hear the low mutter and grunt of men going about some task requiring physical effort. An empty handcart stood outside.

There was no point in concealing his presence any longer. He turned the lamp up and strode forward, through the door, and straight past the generator into the salmon-house. Three faces turned to him in surprise. One of the belonged to Roderick McKay.

Hudson said nothing, only stood noting the scene: one man at the bench, a fine, glistening salmon before him and a knife poised in his hand; another bending over a fish-box, packing it; and Roderick McKay, straightening up from placing empty boxes in readiness.

After the initial surprise, the other two men looked at McKay, as if for an order that might bring them moving menacingly towards the intruder. But McKay gave a slight shake of his head and came forward himself.

'Carry on,' he said over his shoulder. Then, 'I think, Mr Hudson, a word between us in the lodge kitchen would be as well.'

Hudson nodded and lit their way back. Once inside, they stood facing one another across the table, the lamp between them. Keeping his voice low, Hudson commenced.

'So, the Laird of Carnochie comes home by night to die. On a slab, reserved for your employer's fish, taken from his river and shipped away for sale in the market. And a simple wee kitchenmaid half scared out of her wits as a result.'

The bigger man shrugged. ''Tis a pity you chose to poke your nose into the private affairs of this village – a butler from London.'

'I may be a butler, Mr McKay, but I, too, have been a gamekeeper and ghillie in my day; and my father, I'll have you know, was head ghillie to Lord Invermore in Argyllshire for thirty years. My knowledge told me the river here is not a late river.'

'It is a late river – but it has an early spate at this time.'

Hudson nodded. 'I also know that boxes of fish are usually brought ashore from fishing-boats, not loaded on to them and carried away.'

For the first time a flicker of a smile touched McKay's strong mouth. He was a handsome man in his ruggedness, and, momentarily unmasked, seemed a pleasant one.

'Och aye. You're an observant man, Mr Hudson. I'll give you that.'

'Just as well,' Hudson said, 'before the salmon pools were quite emptied by you and your poaching, thieving friends.'

'There's more in the river than a landlord from England needs, coming here only one or two months in a year. It is a waste of good salmon.'

'That's no excuse for theft.'

'Ach, I'm not proud of it, but it's the way we have to make a wee bit extra to live, and the landlord gets his fish a-plenty, just the same. I suppose you will now be sending a telegram to his lordship on his yacht at Monte Carlo – or maybe just fetching the constable?'

Hudson shook his head. 'I'll do neither. To hand you over to the police or your employer at this time will solve nothing. I'll confess I am not over-fond of absentee landlords myself, but nobody has the right to accept a man's money and poach his game. As I see it, Mr McKay, this can be a matter between you, as ghillie to Lord Berkhamstead, and myself, as butler to Lord Bellamy, to be settled in a civilised manner.'

'Aye. It's better that way.'

'Then, sit down, my friend.'

McKay obeyed. Hudson went to a cupboard and returned with a whisky bottle and two glasses. He made no move to open the bottle, though. He leaned forward, completely master of the situation.

'I will pass no judgment on a matter which is none of my business. But I'll tell you this, Mr McKay: when my family, the folk I've served for forty years, come to visit my own country of Scotland, and get cheated, then it is my business. I'll make a gentleman's bargain with you. The fish you have out there now are dead already so they're yours to do with as usual. But tomorrow Major Bellamy will go out and cast a fly on the river, and I very much hope he will catch a salmon. And you will see to it in future that there is dry wood enough for the fires and hot water in the lodge, and that, as I now believe you know would be perfectly possible, the electric generator is in working order. Is that understood?'

'It is as one Scot to another, Mr Hudson. You can depend on it.'

At last Hudson unstoppered the bottle and poised it.

'Then you'll take a wee dram with me, to seal our bargain?'

'Aye, that I will.'

'Good.'

Hudson poured for them both, smiling at last as he did so. When he glanced up to hand McKay his glass, he saw that the ghillie was smiling, too. They drank together.

Next morning was fine, and Mr Hudson contrived to make James accept unsuspiciously that he had been down early to the river and formed the strong opinion that since the heavy rain there might well be salmon in the Carnochie Estate's stretch. James and Georgina went down together with the equipment, and by lunchtime James had landed a fine fish which he let Georgina help him play.

Roderick McKay had come unseen down to the bank to watch them as they brought it in. He nodded approval.

'Well, McKay,' James said triumphantly, 'the fishing's improved rather suddenly, hasn't it?'

Another nod. 'I knew you'd not catch a fish while the rain and the mist were down the hills, sir. It's the climate that's improved – not the fishing.'

James was too preoccupied with success to square up this remark with the ghillie's earlier prophecy.

'I was wondering, sir,' McKay went on, 'whether the young lady and yourself would care to climb up Shielas Tor with me tomorrow morning? There's an eagle's nest, way up on the top there. Maybe you'd care to take a peep at the young ones?'

'Oh, I'd love to!' Georgina said. 'Could I take my camera and photograph them?'

'You could try, miss. It's a fair scramble up the last part of the crag; and we'd need to leave a wee bit early.'

'Early as you like,' James replied happily. 'Breakfast at seven, and boots, eh?'

'That would be as well, sir. I'll bid ye both good-day, then.' With a twitch of a smile, the ghillie went away.

When he was shown the fish, Mr Hudson smiled secretly. He had already noticed that the wood-box in the sitting-room and that in the kitchen had become miraculously full, and that a plentiful pile of kindling and logs lay near the kitchen door. Mrs McKay, too, seemed to have unbent suddenly from a dry, resentful creature to a real help about the house whose first unprompted gesture was to provide a batch of shortbread of her own cooking which evoked cries of pleasure from the servants at teatime. She willingly lent her old book containing the recipe to Mrs Bridges, who sat at the kitchen table that evening copying it in her laborious hand.

As she was doing so, a surge of light swept into the kitchen so suddenly that Mrs Bridges uttered an involuntary cry.

'The light! Electric light at last.'

'Aye,' Mrs McKay said, moving to extinguish the oil lamps. 'McKay has been repairing the generator for you. You'll be doing without the lamps now.'

'Oh my goodness, what a relief. Now, where was I? "Bake in a moderate oven for about half an hour . . .".'

'It might be a wee bit less,' Mrs McKay said.

'Well, if I can make shortbread as good as yours, I'll have learnt something in Scotland.'

'I'll give you a hand with their dinner tonight, Mrs Bridges,' the housekeeper offered for the first time. 'I'll help the lass prepare the vegetables.'

Both Mrs Bridges and Ruby looked quite stunned. If Mrs McKay noticed, she didn't show it.

In the sitting-room, now warm and cheerful under the influence of a lively wood fire and electric light, James, in evening clothes, stood up eagerly as Georgina came in. She was wearing a sleeveless dress of rose-pink chiffon over a silk under-dress, with a flower on the shoulder.

James embraced her, then held her admiringly at arms' length.

'My, you look stunning. I haven't seen that dress before, have I?'

'No. It's new.'

'Are you going to be warm enough?'

'Oh, I'm very hardy now, after a week in the Highlands.'

'Better put on warm clothes in the morning for our climb, though,' he cautioned, releasing her. 'It's bound to be a bit draughty up on the top.'

She nodded and sat on the settee. He hovered near. He had determined to speak out this evening.

'Well, back to London next week, eh? Start making plans.'

Georgina looked up. 'Plans?'

'Our plans. Shall we . . . tell Father tonight?'

She understood suddenly. Her expression showed her alarm and pity.

'Georgina?' he asked, seeing it. 'What's the matter?'

She answered carefully, 'James, I didn't mean . . . when I said the other night . . .'

'You said you loved me.'

'Of course I love you . . .'

'Then . . .'

'. . . in a silly sort of way. I always have loved you. But not like you mean. Not to marry.'

He protested, 'When I said that neither of us seemed to have anyone special in view, you didn't say that wasn't true, and . . . and I thought . . . perhaps . . . at last . . .'

'I should have been more honest, James. Perhaps it was the feeling of this place, being here alone together, miles from anywhere. Coming up here was like going back in time – peat fires and nursery tea and Bonnie Prince Charlie. It's all been a kind of make-believe. But make-believe is for children. We did love each other . . .'

'*Do.*'

'No, did. During the war. But that's all in the past, darling. Can't you see?'

Her heart swelled as she saw his expression crumple and heard him whisper pleadingly, 'Georgina – don't take this away from me. I haven't anything else left.'

Like their last intimate encounter, this, too, was broken abruptly by the entry of Richard, fresh and happy from his break from work and the extra rest, and totally oblivious of the atmosphere into which he had marched. James turned and hid his face in shadow as his father breezed, 'I say, Hudson's been telling me a tradition he got from McKay that Charles Edward Stuart slept here during his wanderings before he sailed for Skye. There's a lock of his hair in a little glass case, somewhere in the house. Mind you, if that unfortunate young man had given every lock of hair that's kept in his memory in Scotland, he'd have been totally bald!'

He noticed that Georgina was clutching her hands about her arms.

'Georgina, my dear, are you cold? That's a rather flimsy dress for this climate, isn't it?'

The muffled voice of James replied, his back still towards them.

'Perhaps a ghost walked over her grave.'

Very contrastingly clad in tweeds and woollen jumper, Georgina came gaily downstairs to the sitting-room early next morning, to find Hudson adjusting the curtains.

'Good morning, Miss Georgina.'

'Good morning, Hudson. Is the Major down yet?'

'I believe he has gone out, miss. Edward went to call him at seven o'clock and found that he had already dressed and left his room.'

'Oh?'

'He left this letter for you in his room, miss.'

Hudson picked up the long white envelope from the small table. She had barely time to rip it open and start unfolding the note when Richard came bustling in. She whipped the letter behind her back.

'Good morning,' Richard said, and kissed her. 'I thought I'd better come and see you safely off, if you're still going with McKay. I'm sorry James won't be with you. He's gone to London.'

'London?'

'He put a note under my door. Apparently he suddenly remembered he'd promised to play in a polo match. Since we're leaving in a few days, anyway, it seemed a pity to miss it.'

'But how did he go?'

'He says he hoped to get a lift on the fishing-boat to Oban and catch the train from there. Sorry if it's spoilt your day, Georgina. You know how impulsive James can be.'

'Yes,' she answered bleakly. 'I know.'

As soon as she was alone she read the note through once, then destroyed it and its envelope. It did not mention polo. It was the old phrases; the old, unwanted sentiments and recriminations of a man who seemed destined never to grow up or to allow himself to settle into any sort of happiness.

She went up the tor with McKay, delighted in the sight of the eaglets, got some photographs which in due course turned out well, and so exhausted herself by the day's efforts that she went to bed early and slept like a log, with never another thought of silly old Jumbo.

A few days later the party took its leave, gravely and courteously seen off by Mr and Mrs McKay.

'I've put the hamper of fish in the taxi,' said the latter to Hudson, aside. 'I would keep it in the carriage with you. I have known salmon taken from the guard's van before now.'

Hudson grinned.

'These poachers get everywhere it seems, Mr McKay.'

'They do indeed, Mr Hudson.'

They shook hands warmly.

CHAPTER FIVE

James Bellamy sailed away not only from Scotland; he sailed from Great Britain altogether. That is not to say that he crossed the Atlantic in that same fishing-boat, nor even that he took a further summary departure without giving any more reason than a fictitious game of polo.

He was on the threshold of middle age, and, in his own eyes and those of the more honest of his limited circle of friends, a failure. He had failed at business, at marriage, at love, and at life. One of his drawers held a medal and ribbon signifying success in war; but only he knew that its real significance was as compensation for gallant effort, rather than success; for injury, rather than triumph.

The decade of the 'Thirties was almost dawning. England, following the unrest of the General Strike and its aftermath, was a place of contrasting bewilderment and escapism, promising nothing, offering little to a drifting, aimless gentleman of comfortable enough financial means but few intellectual or practical ones. It was a time for uncomplicated souls, those who could accept with thankfulness their possession of a job, a home, a family circle; or for those equally uncomplicated, well-off ones, who could find peace of mind in the artificial pleasures of which there were no lack at this time.

So James went to America, to get Georgina and a lot of other things out of his system and to search for the magic elixir which even his disillusionment allowed him to think must eventually come his way. And Georgina, to purge herself of James and of serious emotions of any kind, plunged back into her old social whirl. It meant taking up again with some of the old set whom she had never wished to see again – Dolly Hale, of the film studio debacle, was one of them – but under the influence of jazz music, cigarettes, champagne and childish pranks, personal animosities faded. One took one's companions in their various permutations, and that was all.

'Oh, blast and botheration!' an already slightly squiffy Georgina exclaimed as she unlocked the front door of a darkened No. 165 Eaton Place in the early hours of a summer morning. 'The servants must all be in bed.'

'Don't put the lights on,' hissed Peter Dinmont, close to her elbow. 'Let's play "Murder".' He seized his own female companion in a mock-ferocious grasp. 'Ethel – you are my vict-i-i-im!'

She gave an uncultured cry of genuine fright.

Georgina did put on the hall lights and led the way to the morning-room. Those who followed her were Peter Dinmont and Ethel Kent: he a young gentleman of no other occupation than drawing his allowance from his father and spending it, she a counter assistant at Selfridge's; Dolly Hale and Darrow Morton, an American drifter with literary pretensions; and Robert, Marquis of Stockbridge, a beefy, amiable young man with no positive attributes except his inheritance, and the negative one of being, in the eyes of Georgina, whom he had been escorting during the evening, a wet fish.

For the past few hours they had all been employing their intellects, breeding and education in the noble pursuit known to their time as a 'scavenger hunt'. It required them to acquire between them a number of unrelated objects, ranging from a policeman's helmet and a housemaid's cap to a programme for the Wembley Exhibition and a used tram ticket, and to convey these by dawn or soon after to a certain house in Sussex, where other similarly occupied teams would, they would hope, arrive after them, thus giving them winning status. Then they would all sit down to an enormous, uproarious and still-tipsy breakfast, to fortify themselves for another day of arduous idleness and waste.

'Darrow,' Dolly Hale instructed the American, 'bring the loot in here.'

It was duly poured on to the morning-room carpet.

Darrow Morton asked, 'Where the hell's the helmet?'

'I have it,' said Lord Stockbridge, sheepishly producing it.

When no one else had been able to think of a way of acquiring a policeman's helmet, short of some resort to violence, he had approached a constable with the suggestion that a kitten had got stuck up a tree and had offered to hold the helmet while its owner had climbed up. The ruse had worked, but Stockbridge was not feeling especially proud of himself for it.

'Isn't he sweet?' said Dolly Hale sarcastically.

'I think he was rather clever,' Georgina defended him, making him blush with pleasure.

'I feel a bit guilty,' he admitted. 'That poor devil of a constable might get into trouble.'

'Rot!' exclaimed Darrow, and turned to examine the rest of the booty. 'Say, we don't have a goddam tram ticket!'

'Ow!' said Peter's shop-girl. 'I prob'ly got one in my bag.'

'Such a lucky thing,' Dolly remarked, 'that Ethel happens to travel by tram.'

The ticket was found and Ethel condescendingly congratulated. 'Right,' Darrow said. 'One parlourmaid's cap is all we need.'

'Where do the dear girls sleep?' asked Peter, with an exaggerated leer.

Georgina answered, 'Our parlourmaid's married to the chauffeur, and they live across in the mews. She may have left one of her caps lying around the kitchen, though.'

'Then, we'll all go down and see.'

'Shan't we wake the house?' Robert Stockbridge ventured. Georgina assured him that there was no one presently in residence above stairs, and they pranced off in melodramatic file, Ethel uttering little cries of fear for the beetles they might encounter and Peter squeezing her waist comfortingly.

'Hey!' Darrow cried, almost as soon as the kitchen search had begun. 'I found some aprons. We must be getting warm.'

'They haven't got strings,' Ethel said. 'They're tea-towels.'

'How clever of you to know,' Dolly Hale murmured.

A strange voice froze them all where they stood: 'What is going on here?'

Clad in dressing-gown and pyjamas, Mr Hudson emerged from the servants' hall and stood blinking in astonishment.

'Miss Georgina!'

She smiled guiltily. 'Hello, Hudson. We're on a scavenger hunt, you see. Just looking for something that had to be down here.'

'And which we have now found,' Dolly Hale cried, holding up one of Daisy's white caps. 'Let us repair aloft and celebrate our success with music, dancing and champagne, before we repair hence.'

'Could you bring us a bottle of champagne, please, Hudson?' Georgina requested.

'Make it two,' said the American, Darrow Morton, drily.

'Very good, sir,' Hudson replied, and they trooped away upstairs, only Robert, Marquis of Stockbridge, lingering to murmur to the butler, with whom he was acquainted, 'Sorry to have got you out of bed.'

'That is quite all right, my lord. Thank you.'

The champagne having been served and Hudson ordered back to his bed, the impromptu party swung merrily. Robert, a trifle hesitantly, went up to Ethel Kent and invited her to dance with him to the gramophone music.

'Oh, Lord Stockbridge, thanks ever so!'

'You know who Robert reminds me of?' Darrow confided to Georgina, as they danced past. 'Little Lord Fauntleroy. All lace collars and democracy, being polite to butlers and dancing with shop girls. I'll bet he calls his mother "Dearest".'

'As a matter of fact, he does.'

'Where on earth did you dig her up?' Dolly demanded of Peter.

'Selfridge's, actually.'

'Bargain basement, I suppose.'

When they came together in a dance, Robert said anxiously to Georgina, 'I wouldn't see too much of Darrow Morton, if I were you.'

'Why not?'

'You know . . . drugs. You must have seen how quickly Dolly got lit up earlier this evening, after she'd gone outside with him.'

'What rubbish. Dolly's always changing moods. And I think

it's very bad form to criticise people you're going around with. I can't think why you come, if you disapprove of everything we do.'

'Georgina, that's not fair. I don't mind a bit of fun, but when it comes to risking ruining your life . . .'

'Oh, you're so stuffy. One ought to try everything.'

'Not drugs. Promise me you won't.'

'Promise you? I scarcely even know you, except that you're always hanging round and being a bore. Anyway, we'd better get off to Adele's.'

Georgina swung herself from his hold and cried to them all, 'Come on! Off to Sussex, or we'll lose first prize.'

There was a chorus of assent. The last of the champagne was poured and tossed back, and they meandered out into the night.

'Oh, damn disaster!' Dolly Hale moaned theatrically at first sight of her car. 'Another bloody puncture!'

'We'll have to change the wheel.'

'It's no use. I had a puncture this morning. The spare's still flat.'

'My car's only a two-seater,' Robert said apologetically.

The American suggested, 'Did Lord Bellamy take his car to Wiltshire today?'

'No,' Georgina said. 'They went by train.'

'But how gorgeous, then!' Dolly exclaimed. 'We can borrow it. Clever darling Darrow!'

Robert protested, 'Georgina couldn't take the car without Lord Bellamy's permission.' But Georgina turned on him angrily. 'Why don't you mind your own business? You don't have to do anything daring like coming with us. Come on, the rest of you.'

Discarding all discretion, she led the way across to the mews and up the steps to Edward's and Daisy's flat, and hammered on the door.

'Come on, Edward!' she yelled.

'Open the door – Edward!' Dolly joined in.

Just managing to register that the time was three am, Edward came blearily to the door, startled to see Georgina and seemingly a mob of others there.

'Edward, Lady Dolly's car's got a puncture. We'll have to take ours.'

'Oh . . . Yes, miss. I'll just get dressed.'

'No, it's all right. We'll drive ourselves. If you could just give me the garage key.'

Edward said, as firmly as politeness would permit, 'Excuse me, Miss Georgina, but I don't think his lordship would like anyone but me to drive the car.'

Georgina was as good as prepared to accept this, but Darrow Morton intervened, 'Then there wouldn't be room for all of us.'

'No,' said Dolly from behind. 'I detest crushes, and I absolutely refuse to be squeezed into the back seat with Peter and his shop-girl.'

'Georgina,' Darrow persisted, 'does this car actually belong to your uncle?'

'My guardian? Yes, of course it does.'

'Then what are we all standing around for?' He addressed Edward. 'Would you please fetch the key to the garage?'

'Excuse me, sir, but his lordship is very particular about the car. He doesn't even like her ladyship to drive it without me sitting beside her. I don't think he'd like a stranger to drive it.'

'Oh, don't fuss, Edward,' Georgina said, feeling herself losing face in front of her friends. 'I'll drive it myself.'

'You, Miss Georgina?'

'Look, I promise faithfully that your sacred car shall be touched by no one but myself. That's all right, isn't it?'

Edward had no option but to answer dubiously, 'Yes, Miss Georgina. I'll just get the car out of the garage.'

'Don't worry. We'll see to that,' Darrow insisted. 'Just bring the key.'

'Yes, sir.'

Edward went away. 'Isn't he sweet?' said Dolly, nearly falling backwards down the steps as she wavered and staggered.

The key was fetched and the merry party went excitedly off to claim their prize.

'You shouldn't of let them have it, Eddie,' said Daisy sleepily from the bed.

'What else could I do?' he protested, getting back in, to endure a troubled remainder of the night.

Georgina was not accustomed to driving the Rolls Royce. Getting it out of the garage and through London was tricky. Then Dolly Hale insisted on sitting next to her and shrieking endearments through the open window to the few people about in the pre-dawn streets, waving the policeman's helmet. In the back, Ethel squeaked and giggled as Peter fumbled with her, and Darrow wisecracked with typical American spontaneity.

By the time they had reached Epsom, Georgina was handling the big car with confidence and unconsciously increasing speed. They passed swiftly and gaily through that part of Surrey and then eastward into Sussex, encountering little other traffic moving in either direction. They left the main roads at East Grinstead and meandered along minor ones as they came within ten miles or so of their destination.

It was clear daylight by now and a few more people were stirring. One of them, a village police constable, in shirtsleeves and braces, was pumping up his bicycle tyres against the fence of his cottage. He heard the car, unusually early and fast for that part, and looked up. It swept by, Dolly flourishing the helmet triumphantly at him and calling 'Goodmorning, dahling!'

The policeman didn't smile or wave back. He watched the car out of sight, frowning; and his mind registered its number.

Another early mover was Alf Smith, a cowman whose cottage lay about a mile beyond this village and whose place of employment was another half-mile further still. Day in, day out, Alf Smith's early morning routine was the same: to respond to his alarm clock, dress while the kettle was boiling, make himself a cup of tea and take one to his wife, still abed. Then he would get on his old bicycle and trundle off to get in the cows for milking. A man in his thirties, he had been doing this for eleven years and would likely go on doing it until he was too old to get about.

Or would have done, had not his slightly wobbly emergence from the short lane leading from his cottage coincided with the swoop of the Rolls-Royce over a hump in the narrow lane into which he was riding.

Georgina, horrified, had just quick enough reactions to brake at the moment of impact. But that was too late for Alf Smith. The Rolls screeched to a juddering halt with his bicycle under its front wheels. He himself was flung ahead, to fall spread-eagled face downward in the road. He did not stir.

Robert Stockbridge, following at a safe distance behind the Rolls, drew up near and leaped from his car as soon as it had halted. He ran to the prone figure and made a quick examination. Then he walked back to the Rolls, from which no one had emerged. He looked in at Georgina's side, noting the sprawl of evidently sleeping figures in the back seat.

Georgina and Dolly sat motionless, side by side, their faces frozen with horror. Incongruously, the policeman's helmet still lay in Dolly's lap.

'Where is the car now?' Richard Bellamy, grim-faced, asked Edward later that day. He and Virginia had just returned home, having received a telephone message at their overnight hosts'. An unusually pale Hudson had opened the door to them.

'In Sussex, m'lord,' Edward said, dry-mouthed. 'The . . . the police want it there for the time being.'

'And you didn't drive it there?'

'No, m'lord.'

'Have you any explanation for what happened last night, then?'

'Well, Miss Georgina said she'd be driving, and . . .'

'That is exactly my point. Why was Miss Georgina driving the car, and not you?' Richard was striding up and down in agitation.

'M'lord, she . . . Miss Georgina . . . and some of her friends came along to the mews . . . and it was three o'clock of the morning . . .'

'It makes not the slightest difference what time it was. You are the chauffeur and that car was left in your care. I am very disappointed in you, Edward. I'm afraid I shall have to consider very seriously your position in this household. If Major Bellamy were here . . .'

He broke off as the morning-room doors opened and Mr Hudson ushered in Sir Geoffrey Dillon. Georgina, who had been tidying herself up, after her return by train, came in at the same time. Hudson gestured the resentful Edward out of the room with him.

'I'm afraid I have some bad news,' the lawyer said without preamble. 'The man died two hours ago.'

'Oh, no!'

'There will be an inquest, of course.'

'I won't have to go, will I?' Georgina asked.

'I'm afraid you will. I gather you went to the police station after the accident, and that you all made statements.'

'Yes.'

'What exactly did you yourself say?'

'I . . . I'm not quite sure.'

'But you were driving the car?'

'Yes. I said that. But Darrow said there was absolutely nothing I could have done.'

'Darrow?'

'Darrow Morton. An American friend of Dolly . . . Lady Dolly Hale.'

'Did he say in a statement that there was nothing you could have done?'

'Oh, yes.'

'Then his evidence will clearly be vital. What about the others?'

'Well, they were asleep – apart from Dolly, who didn't seem to remember much. We . . . we'd had quite a lot of champagne, and been up all night. Oh, Robert Stockbridge was there – following in his own car. He was awake – if you call it that.'

'Georgina!' Richard rapped sharply. 'This is no laughing matter. A man has been killed – by a car driven by you.'

But Sir Geoffrey Dillon's look had turned thoughtful, and he made no effort to press the questioning. 'Robert Stockbridge,' he mused. 'The Marquis of Stockbridge? Mm! Now that is more promising, I think.' But he would not say why, and took his departure soon afterward.

In the servants' hall, Edward walked past his wife without a word or a look and tore open the newspaper lying on the long table.

'Oh, no!' she groaned, in pretended exasperation. 'Not another winner that can't lose – only it does!'

For once he didn't joke back. *Situations Vacant*, he answered bitterly. She went to him, but he made no response to her touch on his shoulder.

'Eddie! His lordship hasn't . . . !'

'He's thinking about it. I get the blame for everything in this house, didn't you know? Well, p'raps I'll beat him to it.'

He leaned earnestly forward towards the vacancies columns, but Mr Hudson interrupted him.

'Edward, here is your third class fare to East Grinstead and your bus fare from there. You will collect the car at the police station and then you may have some bread and cheese and a half-pint of light ale before driving back. One-and-ninepence should cover that.'

'Yes, Mr Hudson,' Edward said wearily, folding the paper and putting it down.

'Edward, from all I hear, it would appear that you were entirely blameless in this matter of Miss Georgina and her friends taking the motor car.'

'Huh! Try telling that to his lordship.'

'Don't be impertinent to me, my boy. His lordship is naturally upset. You have to realise that being in service is not unlike being in the army. Our masters, like your officers, are not always right, and they sometimes blame us for things which are not our fault. But we are not expected to answer back, nor to bear grudges, because those are the terms we accept when we enter service.'

Edward's scowl showed his lack of conviction.

'Maybe that's why I didn't like the army, then. A man has

his self-respect, Mr Hudson. I don't reckon he's anything without that.'

But there were those who did not think the same. When Georgina tried to telephone Darrow Morton at his hotel she was told that he had left there at very short notice, presumably upon some urgent summons back to the United States, for his baggage had been forwarded to Southampton.

Dolly Hale's telephone rang and rang for days, but was never answered. Georgina was trying her yet again when Peter Dinmont was shown into the morning-room.

'Thank goodness for someone!' she exclaimed. 'What'll you have to drink?'

'Er, well, nothing, thanks. I can't stay, Georgina. I just called in to wish you good luck for the inquest. It's tomorrow, isn't it?'

'Of course. But you'll be there, won't you? And Ethel?'

'Well, no, they . . . they haven't called me. They have my statement. I . . . Ethel and I . . . we didn't see anything, so . . .'

'But at least you were in the car. You could say I wasn't driving recklessly. I wasn't drunk.'

'Oh, well, actually, I don't really remember much . . . We were a bit squiffy, you know – and then we went to sleep. Look, Georgina, I'm awfully sorry, but you see, though Ethel's a decent sort and all that, if it came out that I was out with a girl like that . . . I mean, my father does get pretty ratty about what he calls unsuitable girls. And being on an allowance does make it dashed awkward. I hope you see.'

'I see,' Georgina said. 'Thanks, Peter.'

'Awfully sorry,' he mumbled, getting up and going.

So, she was to be on her own. The thought of Robert Stockbridge never so much as entered her mind. If it had, she would probably have dismissed it. But it had not escaped Sir Geoffrey Dillon's mind. He came bustling round to Eaton Place on the morning of the inquest. Richard and Virginia were in the morning-room, waiting for Georgina to come down and join them for the drive to Sussex, where the hearing would be held as close to the scene of the accident as was feasible.

'I thought we arranged to meet down there,' Richard said, surprised.

'We did. But I wanted a word with your first, Richard, Lady Bellamy. I thought you ought to know that Lord Stockbridge will not be giving evidence.'

'But he must!' exclaimed Virginia, who had heard of the defections of all the others.

The lawyer shook his head in his enigmatic way.

'I have just heard from the Buckminster solicitor. The Duke is very anxious that his son should not appear, and Lord Stockbridge is down in the country.'

Richard objected. 'But surely you could have insisted. He'd have given evidence for us.'

'I understand that the Duke has had a word with the Chief Constable, pointing out that Lord Stockbridge was not actually involved in the accident. In the circumstances, I didn't feel it would be advisable to intervene. The hearing will, ah, receive much less publicity without the unwelcome notoriety of a duke's eldest son giving evidence.'

He gave Richard his unemotional stare.

'I see,' Richard said. 'Well, then, are you coming in our car?'

'No, thank you. I have my own. I'll see you there.'

He went out. Virginia asked anxiously, 'But why? Why on earth . . . ?'

Richard smiled. 'My dear, I'm sure it's for the best. I've lived long enough to recognise a deal when I see it – or perhaps I should say, when I smell it. In this case, between two solicitors, who've reached a compromise. One might as well try to break an agreement between a couple of horse-dealers. In any case, there'd be nothing to gain. Ah, Georgina, my dear. All ready?'

And, more sedately, on this occasion, with the still unhappy Edward at the wheel, the Rolls-Royce repeated its journey down into Sussex, to a village hall where a coroner, a jury, lawyers, witnesses and public awaited with emotions of varying intensity, or no emotion at all, the coming of the beautiful, unnaturally pale young woman who was to be the centre of their attention.

The widow of Alfred Henry Smith was the first to stand up before the coroner, the local doctor. He had known her for years, and poor Alf Smith; but the formalities had to be observed.

'Mrs Smith, you have identified your husband?'

She nodded through tears.

'I don't want to upset you, Mrs Smith, but there are one or two questions I must ask. Your husband worked as cowman at Penfold Farm?'

A mumbled, 'Yes, sir.'

'Please speak up a little. Now, when did you last see him – alive?'

'Last Tuesday marning, sir. As usual, he'd set the alarm clock and put it on the biscuit-tin – to make more sound, you see, sir, being a heavy sleeper – and when it went off he says, "It's larmentable cold," he says, "but I reckon it'll be a purty day later." Then he brought me my tea and then he says, "Cheerio," and that was the . . . the last . . .'

Tears welled up more strongly. The coroner looked enquiringly across at Sir Geoffrey Dillon, clearly hoping to spare the witness any further questioning, but Dillon was rising to his feet, with an air of regret.

'Mrs Smith,' he said gently, 'you say your husband was a heavy sleeper. Did he oversleep on this particular morning.'

'Well . . . not exactly oversleep, sir.'

'How do you mean, please?'

'Well, after the alarm had run down I had to call him once or twice.'

'So he did oversleep.'

'Only by a minute or two, sir. He wasn't never late to work, not in all the days we was married. Mr Penfold'll bear me out in that.'

The farmer nodded vigorously. The coroner addressed Sir Geoffrey. 'I really don't see what . . .'

'I was merely trying to establish whether perhaps Mr Smith

was conscious of being later than usual, and was endeavouring to, er, hurry, consequently not riding with quite his usual attention.'

'Mrs Smith,' the coroner asked, 'did your husband ride a modern, high-speed bicycle?'

'No, sir. It was an old iron one what had belonged to my father. "Quite an old friend," he used to say.'

Sir Geoffrey looked interested at this.

'Do you know when Mr Smith last had the brakes attended to on this old bicycle?' he asked.

'Well, I don't know as he ever . . . I mean, he used to tinker with it himself, now and then.'

'Did the brakes actually work at all?'

'He . . . he did used to say they wasn't all that good, but they was all right for round here.'

Sir Geoffrey was nodding his thanks and sitting down, to the coroner's relief. Mrs Smith was released with the Court's expression of sympathy and Police Constable Burridge took her place. He deposed that he had been called to an accident at the foot of the hill known at Carter's Rise, where he had found the Rolls-Royce, the mangled bicycle and the unconscious Alfred Smith. He had recognised the car as one he had seen some minutes earlier.

'Why was that?' the coroner wanted to know.

'It went through the village at high speed, sir. There was a woman leaning out of the window, waving a policeman's helmet.'

'Did you recognise this person?'

'Not at the time, sir, but I later discovered it was that lady over there – Lady Dorothy Hale. I reckoned they'd all been drinking quite a bit.'

'And it was undoubtedly this same car which shortly afterwards was involved in the accident which killed Mr Smith?'

'Yes, sir.'

'Sir Geoffrey?'

'Constable, we have heard from Mrs Smith that her husband was bicycling to work at Penfold's Farm. Now, to reach the farm he would have had to travel directly across the highway from the point at which he emerged.'

'Yes, sir.'

'Is there a great deal of traffic on that road?'

'Very little at all, 'specially at that time of the morning.'

'So Mr Smith would be unlikely to be expecting a car to come along?'

'No, sir.'

'Someone driving a car cannot, in fact, see the foot of Carter's Rise until they are over it.'

'That's correct, sir.'

'Exactly. So we can imagine Mr Smith, on his old and not altogether reliable bicycle, on which it would perhaps be difficult to brake, or turn, or increase speed suddenly in any emergency – we can picture him riding out on to the highway in the path of this oncoming car, whose driver would have had no warning of his presence on the road.'

'That is pure supposition, Sir Geoffrey,' the coroner intervened.

'But it is a supposition which it is very reasonable to make,' the lawyer answered blandly. He turned again to the witness. 'Now, you say you "reckoned" that the occupants of the car had been drinking. Would you not agree that what in fact you observed could have been simply a party of high-spirited young people enjoying themselves in the exhilaration of a country outing?'

A murmur of objection rose from the public seats and the coroner frowned as he reflected it officially. 'Come, come, Sir Geoffrey. I think the constable is as capable as the rest of us of judging whether or not people have been drinking.'

Sir Geoffrey's imperturbable answer was to sit down, leaving the point undisputed.

'Laughing and shouting?' the coroner asked Georgina, after she in turn had described their progress that fatal morning. Sir Geoffrey Dillon protested, but was ignored in his turn. 'You were in high spirits,' the coroner pressed.

'We'd been to a party,' Georgina admitted with a matter-offactness which did nothing to please the locals.

'At what speed do you say you were travelling, Miss Worsley?'

'I really couldn't say. But then, suddenly, this man on a bicycle came out of a side turning, right in front of the car. I put the brakes on, but . . .' She broke off and shrugged in a gesture of helplessness.

The coroner looked at Sir Geoffrey Dillon, who merely stared back as if the other were invisible. The foreman of the jury took his chance to speak up for his restless colleagues.

'Sir, we'd like to ask the young lady if she thinks it's right that an honest working man can't go about his business without getting knocked down and killed by a lot of titled people driving about the countryside because they've got nothing better to do.'

Before Sir Geoffrey could object the coroner had ruled the question out of order. Then Darrow Morton was called and found to have left the country; and Dolly Hale made what could only be termed an appearance, irritating the coroner and riling the locals by her flippant and patronising answers to the questions. Richard Bellamy gripped his wife's hand tightly as both realised what sort of an impression of herself and her set Dolly was conveying to the jury and the few members of the Press; an impression that could only tarnish Georgina, too.

Dillon shrewdly cut short his examination of this unsatisfactory witness and the coroner prepared to give his summary of what had been heard in his court. But he had to pause as a constable hurried in with a note for Sir Geoffrey Dillon. Sir Geoffrey rose and begged for a moment's indulgence. Granted it, he went to the back of the room where a beefy young man stood. They argued briefly, after which Sir Geoffrey, with clear reluctance, returned to his place and the young man came forward towards the witness stand.

'May I ask what is happening?' said the coroner. 'Who is this?'

P.C. Burridge, sitting close by, enlightened him: 'It's the

gentleman who fetched me to the scene of the accident, sir. The Marquis of Stockbridge.'

'Yes,' Robert Stockbridge acknowledged. 'I'd like to give evidence, please.'

The coroner shook his head. 'No, no, you can't, I'm afraid. We've finished the hearing.'

'But I was driving just behind. I saw the accident.'

'Even so . . . Oh, very well, Lord Stockbridge. You had better tell us what you know of this affair. Wait a moment, though. You'll have to take the oath first.'

Robert Stockbridge did, and then explained: 'I was driving close behind Miss Worsley's car. I reached the top of the hill and saw her travelling down at about thirty miles an hour. I know that was the speed, because I'd just glanced at my speedometer and I continued to travel at the same distance behind her. I saw a man on a bicycle ride straight out in front of the car from a side lane. There was nothing anyone could have done.'

A silence fell on the room. The coroner looked at the jury, who looked at one another. Richard looked at Virginia, who looked at him. Georgina looked with astonishment at Robert Stockbridge, standing soldierly to attention and staring in front of him. Sir Geoffrey Dillon's eyes never left the papers on the school desk at which he sat.

The first sound before the murmur of general reaction came was the sobbing of the dead man's widow. Whatever mattered to anyone else, only one thing concerned her; and that thing was beyond all practical concern, anyway.

She scarely heard the verdict of accidental death and the coroner's endorsement of the jury's rider to the effect that the irresponsible behaviour of Miss Georgina Worsley and her friends had been a contributory factor in the fatal occurrence. No alarm clocks on any biscuit tins would ever wake her Alf again.

'Oh, that is a relief!' Mrs Bridges declared, when Mr Hudson had read out the verdict from the evening newspaper.

'Fancy the paper getting it in so soon, though,' Daisy said.

'I imagine they had a journalist in court, and he telephoned an account of it to London,' Hudson replied, still reading to himself.

'What is it, Mr Hudson?' Mrs Bridges asked, seeing him frown suddenly.

' "Coroner Rebukes Bright Young People",' he quoted the sub-heading. They looked at one another.

At that moment Eddie came in, jerking open the top button of his uniform jacket and tossing his peaked hat on to the table. He barely acknowledged his wife, let alone the rest of them.

'What was it like in court, Edward?' Mrs Bridges asked. He answered rudely, 'How should I know? I was left outside, minding their precious car.'

'Edward!' Mr Hudson rebuked him, but Edward's thoughts had festered beyond the limits of discipline.

'No,' he said. 'I been thinking about what happened the other day. I've always been second-best in this household, and now this talk of giving me the sack, without a chance to defend myself . . .'

'Edward, I myself explained to you the position . . .'

'Yeah, but you're not his lordship, are you? You're just the butler, and I'm just the chauffeur. Well, I've had enough.'

'What about me?' Daisy asked.

He had thought about that. 'You can stay on here if you want. Go back into your old room. I'll go to Mum's, till I find another place for us both.'

'Oh, Eddie, I know he's hurt your feelings, but . . .'

'Yes, he has.'

'Oh, well . . . You must do what you think right, love.'

'I'm going to, Dais.'

But not many minutes passed before Edward was summoned to the morning-room.

'Might as well get it over with,' he remarked, doing up his buttons again as he went up the stairs from the servants' hall. But he was put off his stride by his lordship's expression as he greeted him in the morning-room.

'Edward, Miss Georgina asked me to speak to you. I was going to in any event. I understand now that you did everything you could to prevent the car from being taken without you that night. From all I hear, you were placed in a very difficult position, and I'm only sorry that when I spoke to you about it I gave you no chance to explain. I hope you will accept my apology, here and now.'

He thrust out his hand with a smile. Edward could do no more than accept it, stammering thanks, and take his leave.

'His lordship apologised!' Daisy exclaimed when he told her. 'Then it's all right, isn't it?'

'Yeh, I suppose so. It's not like the old days, though, is it?'

'How d'you mean?'

'Lady Marjorie wouldn't never have apologised. She'd never have needed to in the first place.'

'Oh, come on and eat your tea. It's haddock.'

'I don't like haddock.'

In the background, Mrs Bridges and Mr Hudson exchanged glances. It was becoming less and less like the old days, it seemed.

CHAPTER SIX

'There they are, then,' said Mrs Bridges, sprinkling cress decoratively around the sandwiches of smoked salmon and thin brown bread. 'Daisy, just moisten that cover and lay it over them in case of flies. Then you can take them up, with the wine chilled just right, as soon as Miss Georgina gets in. I must say, she's taken a real passion for smoked salmon lately.'

Daisy smirked. 'Or Lord Stockbridge has.'

'What's that? What are you insinuating now, Daisy?'

'Nothing, 'cept that it's him has taken her out for the third time in a fortnight.'

'One swallow doesn't make a summer.'

'Mebbe not, but three might. If you ask me, they're walking out proper.'

'Well, it's high time that girl did settle down after one thing and another. Oh, this heat! My ankles is swollen up like bolsters. I think I shall just sit down for a few minutes. You keep a sharp ear for Miss Georgina, in case I just happen to drop off for a second or two.'

'All right, Mrs B.'

Georgina Worsley was not a young lady of many sensibilities. Pleasure and idleness made up her everyday routine, and she felt no urge to change her ways. No ambition nagged at her. Unlike her cousin James Bellamy, still away in America, she knew nothing of frustration and thwarted endeavours. She changed her male escorts almost as often as she changed frocks; or had done until the aftermath of the motoring tragedy.

Her generally impervious emotional skin had been pierced by Robert Stockbridge's gallant defence of her. At a time when all the people she had called her friends had left her to face the ordeal of the inquest alone, the man she had scorned to his face for his insipidity had voluntarily spoken up for her, in defiance of his parents' orders. The act had both touched and impressed Georgina. Robert, now, appeared to her not wet, but gentle. He no longer seemed beefy, but well-made. His attentions were no longer a bore, but a pleasure. For once, Georgina allowed herself to be monopolised by one man; and that man was only too delighted and eager to see her as often as possible.

On this day he had taken her down to his old school, Eton, for the Fourth of June celebrations. The year was 1929, a year of worry and unrest. While Etonians celebrated, more than a million other males queued for jobs or dole, or lounged aimlessly at street corners. The Prime Minister, Stanley Baldwin, puffed phlegmatically at his pipe, smiled his kindly smile, and did nothing, as a result of which the desperate electorate turned out in the greatest numbers ever known to vote his government out of office and give the Labour Party its first real chance to show what it could do, under the leadership of Ramsay Macdonald and a policy of nationalisation and heavy taxation of riches.

Richard Bellamy would no longer be a minister. It did not trouble him unduly. He had served his country faithfully for many years, and would go on serving it in the House of Lords. Although he remained healthy and upright, his looks belying his age by many years, he knew nowadays much more about the meaning of tiredness and strain than in bygone years.

He and Georgina were the only upstairs occupants of No. 165 Eaton Place at present. Virginia was away in Scotland. Mr Hudson's and Rose's holidays had been fixed to coincide with her absence, leaving only Mrs Bridges, Edward and Daisy, and, like a kitchen fixture or implement, Ruby.

Mrs Bridges did doze off for a few minutes. She woke with a start as the morning-room bell rang.

'There they are, Daisy. Take them their wine and sandwiches, and ask if there's anything else they'd like.'

Daisy obeyed. She found Georgina looking at her most radiant, the almost transparent skin glowing from the sun and fresh air. Lord Stockbridge was pink and boyishly beaming. Daisy served the snack, was told there was nothing else required, and departed.

'Tuck in,' Georgina told Robert, 'or you might not get any. I'm famished.'

They ate and drank enthusiastically.

'And thank you for a marvellous day,' she said sincerely. 'I shall always bless old Henry the Sixth for founding Eton on the fourth of June.'

'Dear old Henry,' Robert grinned. 'He'd get a shock now if he could see the result of his labours. All those little scruffs in top hats.'

'I wish I'd been a boy and gone to Eton. Rowing on the Thames on a lovely summer's day. Not like being at school at all.'

'I didn't do much rowing, actually. I was a "dry bob". I played cricket.'

'Were you good at it?'

'Not too bad. I actually got into the Eleven.'

'Do you still play?'

He didn't answer. She looked up, to find him regarding her with an unaccustomed intensity. She smiled affectionately. 'I asked if you still play?'

'Eh? Oh, yes. Yes, I do. For the village team. They've made me captain, though Frank Bowman, our postman, does all the work really. He runs the team, does the fixtures, mows the pitch . . . He's also our demon bowler, and his brother Joe, the blacksmith, keeps wicket. When Joe hits a six it's like a great firework going up. My father still plays sometimes. He creaks a bit fielding, but the Duke's donkey drops are always treated with becoming respect.'

'What's a donkey drop?'

'When you bowl a ball very high, and it comes down almost on the stumps. Quite tricky when the sun's in the right place . . . Georgina . . . Darling Georgina . . . I do love you, you know.'

This switch from boyish gabble to seriousness surprised her by its suddenness. She could make no reply before he went on.

'I love you. I absolutely adore you. I started to fall in love with you ages ago and now I think about you all the time.'

'Could . . . could I have some more wine, please?' she

managed to ask, in something of a daze. He poured for her. 'Why didn't you tell me before?'

'I think it was because I was so terrified you'd say no. You . . . aren't going to, are you?'

The frank immediacy of her reply staggered him.

'No.'

'You mean, "yes"? You mean . . . you actually love me, too!'

'Yes.'

'It's . . . it's marvellous. Incredible! If you'd turned me down I don't know what I'd have done. I couldn't live without you, Georgina.'

'Please don't say that, Robert.'

'But it's true. I . . .'

'But please don't say it. Someone said it to me once before. Someone very nice – but I didn't love him, and he shot himself. I suppose I'm just superstitious, really. He'd been in the war and wasn't quite . . . James has never got over the war, you know. He has rages and terrible miseries still. I'm glad you weren't touched by the war, Robert.'

'Only by the lousy food we had at school.'

'It was just after that I decided I didn't want to get mixed up with anyone again. Just going to endless parties, and acting in that film, and behaving like a lunatic. I suppose I was trying to keep real life at bay. It was quite fun, though, being one of the Bright Young Things.'

'Didn't you ever suspect that I would ask you to marry me?'

She looked at him wryly. 'You haven't, actually.'

He flung himself down into the Victorian suitor's pose, one knee bent, hand on heart.

'Miss Worsley, will you do me the great honour of consenting to be my wife?'

'I shall have to think about it, Lord Stockbridge,' she replied primly, but smiled her reassurance when she saw the little shadow of anxiety which passed over his features. It was quickly gone. He sat beside her again.

'Do you think your guardian will approve?' he asked.

'Yes. What about your parents?'

He hesitated, ever so slightly, before answering, 'They'll adore you. Of course they will.'

She didn't notice the hesitation. Neither did it occur to her that the expression of reassurance might have been more for Robert's own benefit than for hers.

He drew her to him and, for the first time in many years, she joined in a kiss with sincerity and genuine love.

'My people are away in Austria at the moment,' he said at length. 'They'll be back next week. It's nearly Ascot and we've got a house party at Shalford. I hope you'll come and stay as soon as possible and meet my parents.'

'I'd love to, Robert.'

'The old place is far too big nowadays, but I hope we'll always hang on to it. Just think . . . in about a hundred years' time you and I will be having tea by the lake, surrounded by hundreds of grandchildren. The old Duke and the old Duchess.'

'What a thought!'

'I must show you a painting I did of Shalford. Give you some impression.'

'I didn't know you painted. Do you do it a lot?'

'Hardly at all, actually. Father isn't too keen on it. He seems to think it's rather . . . well, not quite the thing for a gentleman. One of our neighbours has four sons and one of them paints professionally. Father always refers to them as "three good boys and an artist".'

'Well, when we're married we'll have a studio for you in our London house.'

He gave his boyish smile again. 'That's what I've always wanted. And to go and paint in Paris and Florence and Venice.'

'You shall, darling. Precious few people have any talent at all. You must use yours.'

'I suppose so. I'm rather an idle sort of person, really. It's terribly easy just to mooch around and do nothing in particular, rather like my father and grandfather did when they were young – except they had wars and things to keep them occupied.'

'Thank goodness you're not going to have a war to keep you occupied.'

He nodded seriously, then smiled again. 'I'll have to rely on you to kick me around. Keep me busy. Anyway, I suddenly feel life's worth living, now I've got you. I mean, there's some point in it which there never was before. We have a party, we'll have it because we want to see our friends, not because we're bored and there's nothing else to do. Let's care immensely for the things we mind about and chuck the rest out of the window.'

'Yes, please!'

Richard responded to the news exactly as Georgina had confidently predicted. Robert delivered it in the formal manner, requesting permission to marry Georgina and receiving a warm handshake and a slap on the shoulder in response. But Robert's slight hesitation in assuring Georgina that his own parents would be equally delighted had not been without significance. He telegraphed them in Vienna but received no reply. They returned to London two days later and Robert found himself duly summoned to his mother's presence.

The Duchess of Buckminster was in her early fifties but had had at least a decade of her life restored by expensive grooming and dressing. She was trim of figure, elegant of carriage and gesture, memorable of features, exact down to the last hair and touch of make-up – and as conscious of her authority as any woman who ever combined beauty, position and wealth.

Robert, standing before her expensively furnished desk in her own sitting-room, felt like a schoolboy being called to account by a smiling yet severe headmistress.

'It did come as rather a shock to us, darling . . . just getting your telegram out of the blue.'

'Yes, I . . . I see that. But I thought I'd better let you know . . . well, as soon as I knew.'

'I quite see that. What surprised us, though, was that you hadn't introduced Miss Worsley to us before.'

'Well, you haven't met a lot of my friends. I mean, why should you?'

The headmistress's tolerant smile diminished somewhat. 'This is rather more than a friend, I gather.'

Robert clenched and unclenched his hands. 'I'm sorry, Mother. I didn't really think of it before. I mean, I didn't really know I was going to marry her.'

'You mean you had no idea?'

'Of course I had. But I didn't know what she would say. I could hardly tell you before I'd asked her, could I?'

'*Tell* us? I just wish you hadn't taken us quite so much by surprise, Robert.' She saw his gesture of exasperation. 'You know exactly what I mean.'

'I think so,' he said, the irritation sounding. 'Do I take it from all this that you and Father are against my getting married?'

'Of course not, darling. Only, it is a tremendously important step in your life, and after all the unfortunate publicity over that inquest last year . . .'

'So that's it!'

'. . . after all that, you can hardly expect us to be greatly enthusiastic that you've chosen Miss Worsley. Your father was extremely cross when you deliberately went against his express wishes, you know.'

'Mother, I had to give evidence at that inquest. Georgina might have gone to prison if I hadn't.'

'I think that most unlikely.'

'Anyway, don't let's go all over that again. It's over and done with. When you get to know Georgina you'll change your mind, I'm sure.'

'We don't know her yet, of course – but we do know of her.'

'What exactly do you mean by that, Mother?'

'I mean she is . . . quite a well-known young lady. She seems to get her face in the papers quite a lot.'

'Only because she enjoys doing original things, and happens to be very beautiful. I don't think you can blame her for that.'

The immaculate Duchess sighed, and smiled wistfully. 'You must believe me, my darling, that your father and I only want what is best for you. Your future happiness is terribly important to all of us. You will admit it has all been . . . rather sudden.'

'I don't admit anything of the sort.'

'Oh, do be reasonable, Robert!'

'I'm being perfectly reasonable.'

'Darling, we only think you should give it time. Think about it, so that you're quite, quite sure.'

Robert, who had been shuffling to and fro across the carpet in growing irritation, exploded in a manner worthy of his father.

'Don't you think I've thought about it . . . endlessly . . . for hours and hours? And you talk about giving it time! Heavens above, I love the girl and she loves me. We want to get married. Isn't that enough?'

His mother touched her perfectly set hair. There was a little tinkle of bracelets as her hand moved.

'No, darling. I don't think it is.'

Robert wanted to telephone Georgina as soon as this painful interview was over, but he remembered just in time that she was acting as hostess to her uncle at an important function and decided not to disturb her. He called on her next day. She received him in her room, where she and Daisy were sorting through some clothes. She dismissed her maid and turned anxiously to Robert's clouded face.

'You've seen your parents,' she said, more in the manner of a statement than a question.

'Not Father. He went straight down to Shalford. I knew that was a bad sign, for a start. I've had a blinding row with Mother. Oh, damn it, they're being utterly prejudiced and idiotic.'

'You mean, they don't approve,' said Georgina, who had been not unprepared for the news.

'For the most ridiculous reasons. I haven't introduced you. You're "notorious". Good God . . . !'

'Well, I suppose if you look at it from their point of view, you are quite a catch, darling. I mean, they probably think I've been chasing you and once I've got my tiny claws into you I won't let go until you marry me.'

'Damn her! Damn them both, that's all I can say!'

'It's no good saying that,' she said. 'I wish I could just meet them.'

'I know. They're so damned prejudiced. But they don't own me, you know. I'm not going to "think again", Georgina. I shan't let you down.'

He seized her hands and clutched them hard. She asked, with real curiosity. 'Would this be the first time you'd . . . defied them?'

Robert looked surprised. 'I suppose it will,' he said slowly. 'The first important time.'

There was a knock at the door. They stood apart and Daisy entered, carrying a small silver salver. Robert recognised the brand of pink envelope it bore, and the large, sloping handwriting addressing it to Georgina.

When she had read it she handed it to him.

'There you are,' she said happily. 'Your mother's asked me to tea tomorrow.'

Robert read the note. The expression on his face didn't match Georgina's, though.

The Duchess greeted Georgina with the utmost graciousness, thanking her profusely for taking the trouble to call and see her, sending the liveried footmen at once for tea and pouring it herself when the butler had brought it. Georgina could imagine that the tray, the silver, the porcelain were all priceless. She was being given the first-class grade of reception, which seemed to augur very well. The nervousness she had brought with her began to recede.

'I'm sorry we haven't had the chance to meet before,' the Duchess smiled, proffering another of the delicious sandwiches. 'I had lunch with Lady Berkhamstead yesterday. She said you were a nurse in the war.'

'Yes, I was. I tried to do something, like everyone else.'

'She said you were a very good one. And how is Major Bellamy? My brother was with him in the Life Guards, you know. He was killed, sadly.'

'Oh, James is in America. From his letters, he's enjoying himself and doing quite well. Financial dealings, you know. He's hoping to come back to see us this autumn.'

'Really? Have you been to America, Miss Worsley?'

'Yes, once. I enjoyed it.'

'I expect you went to Hollywood, to make films.'

It did not escape Georgina's notice that the Duchess had evidently been doing some thorough research into her background.

'No,' she answed. 'I went to stay with James's sister Elizabeth. I'm afraid my film experience has been rather exaggerated. I've only been in one, and that was just for fun.'

'You young people do have a great deal of fun nowadays. So much freedom compared to my time as a girl. One hears of all sorts of people doing all sorts of things. I suppose it's good really, but they don't seem to stick at any one thing much, do they? I'm afraid that's rather typical of Robert, too . . . He doesn't seem able to stick at anything.'

'He tells me he's very keen to paint.'

'Oh, yes. He really has a talent. I remember how proud I was when he won a prize at school . . . but he hasn't kept up with it really.'

Georgina ventured to ask, 'Has he really been given the chance?'

The Duchess's smile didn't wane. 'Oh Lord, yes. But, as I say, he doesn't stick at things. He was up at Oxford but left after a year or so. Never took his degree – not that he needed one particularly. Robert's a charming, easygoing person and my husband and I love him dearly. But people with that sort of nature can make so many mistakes in life . . .'

She let the sentence die away and poured them both more tea. Then she smiled winningly at Georgina again.

'You're a very pretty girl, my dear. Much prettier than your photographs. I'm sure lots of men must have fallen in love with you.'

'Well, plenty have said they were. Some of them asked me to marry them, but I've never accepted anyone . . . before. I didn't love them, and I do love Robert. I think he's the sort of person who will never let me down.'

'I'm sure he wouldn't let anyone down . . . not deliberately, anyway.'

Georgina shook her head. 'Not in any way. I haven't met anyone quite like him before.'

'It's very nice of you to say so.'

There was a pause. Georgina sensed that the next word must be from the Duchess, and that the critical moment of the interview had been reached. She was not wrong.

'We've decided,' the Duchess said, matter-of-factly, 'that the best thing for Robert would be to go abroad for a few months.'

Georgina's mouth almost dropped open. This was a decision whose possibility had not remotely occurred to her. It was quite a shock. The Duchess was continuing, 'My husband has arranged it all. He'll be going all over the world. During that time we don't want you to see each other. You seem a sensible girl, and I hope you'll help us persuade Robert to do as we wish. If you love each other as you say you do, it will make no difference in the long run.'

'I think that's unfair,' Georgina said boldly. Her effrontery didn't seem to put the Duchess out at all, though. She continued, as if she were wearing her coronet as she spoke: 'Robert is our only son. He is very dear to us indeed. He's also heir to a great inheritance. I don't mean just titles. I mean, land, responsibility to people, thousands of people. We don't think he's quite ready to take on that responsibility . . . not that he will have to, we hope, for some time. And we don't think he's quite ready to get married.'

She got up, timing it perfectly. Georgina rose automatically.

'I don't expect you to agree with me,' the Duchess said, 'or even to understand why I seem to be behaving like a fussy old hen. But at least I thought I owed you an explanation.'

She pressed the bell beside the fireplace.

'Thank you,' was all Georgina could find to say.

'Not at all. I've so much enjoyed meeting you.'

The footman was holding open the door. Georgina obediently took her leave.

'I'll write every day, wherever you are,' Georgina assured Robert when they met for the last time. 'And you must promise to have a good time. It'll be a great experience for you. You can find all sorts of exciting places to take me when we're married.'

Her initial disappointment had given way to resignation and then to a sort of contentment. She had consulted her Uncle Richard, who had pointed out that the bargain implied by the Duchess of Buckminster was a pretty fair and satisfactory one, and, looked at objectively, a sensible one, too. If Georgina and Robert's love survived the few months of separation and they had faithfully obeyed the condition imposed on them, then they could not reasonably be refused their reward. If it didn't survive so simple a test, then they could both feel they had had a lucky escape from a great mistake. He advised Georgina to ask herself how she would have spent the next few months anyway, had no such prospect existed. As things stood, she could live as usual, but with the exception of a happy end to the aimless drifting which no longer held any attraction for her.

She kissed him and thanked him, and went off positively glowing with satisfaction.

Robert found it harder to accept the situation philosophically.

'I still think I'm being damned weak, giving in to them like this,' he grumbled. 'If I want to marry you, why shouldn't I?'

'Darling, you will. I'll be here for you.'

'Yes, but the waste of all those months . . .'

She laid a finger to his lips.

'We've been through it all so often. I tell you what. Let's plan a date to get married. Then it'll feel so positive and I can cross off every day in my diary.'

She got her little diary out of her bag and consulted it.

'June next year,' Robert said at a hazard.

Georgina examined the date chart. 'June the twelfth,' she chose. 'A Thursday.'

Robert grinned, happy now. 'Thursday, June the twelfth, 1930. That's going to be a day when history is made.'

'Goodbye, my love,' Georgina said when they had kissed, long and lingeringly.

He left her. She sat down with the open diary still in her hand, staring at the rows of figures which tabulated the future.

It was, of course, her own and Robert's future which concerned her solely at that moment. She did not plague her fancy with anyone else's – which perhaps was just as well.

CHAPTER SEVEN

James returned from New York in October. He was little changed, apart from some becoming graying of his hair and a tendency to use an occasional Americanism in his speech, which had always been so precisely English.

Unfortunately, it was not long in becoming apparent that his manner had not changed, either. He answered Mr Hudson's enquiry as to whether he had had a pleasant voyage by saying that there had been too many people jostling about on the ship for his comfort. He grimaced when informed that Richard and Virginia had been unable to stay in to receive him, having had to attend an official reception at the unlikely venue of Madame Tussaud's waxworks, and that Georgina was out visiting Robert Stockbridge's aunt, Lady Isobel Dawson.

He was offered tea, but rather brusquely ordered a bath instead. An atmosphere of anti-climax seemed to attend his homecoming.

There was even a hint of sarcasm, although it was overlaid with raillery, in his questioning of Georgina that evening about Robert Stockbridge. She had greeted him with a fond kiss and embrace and told him how good it was to have him back.

'You don't need me, by all accounts,' he replied. 'Anyway, congratulations, if they're still in order. Here. This is for you.'

'This' was a fur which must have matched in expense the emerald necklace he had just presented to Virginia and the more masculine gift he had brought his father.

'Oh, James, it's wonderful! Thank you so much.'

'I hope your intended takes it in the right spirit.' He turned to Richard. 'Is this fellow as splendid as she makes out in her letters?'

'Well, I'm very fond of him myself. We all are.'

'Hm. Bit Victorian, isn't it? Sending a fellow half way round the world to get rid of him.'

'Tell that to the Duke,' Georgina said with feeling. 'Persuade him to let him come back to me.'

They went in to dinner. As she had always done on James's first day back from school or any other prolonged absence, Mrs Bridges had cooked Spotted Dick for pudding to follow the pheasant. He appreciated the wine more.

'Chateau Lafite. Excellent. I haven't tasted anything like it in two years. Prohibition must be the maddest law ever passed.'

Georgina said, 'When I was there, rich people broke it all the time.'

'Oh, everyone breaks it now. They fight over it. I was nearly killed in a riot in Phoenix.'

'You never told us that!'

'Well, naturally. Elizabeth and Dana keep their liquor in a dug-out in the garden. I must say, she's in her element. One of the most talked-about hostesses in New York. The house is jam-packed with politicians, writers, the best society. But the brokers are the real lions of the moment. The talk's all money.'

'How boring,' Virginia said.

'No, you don't understand. It's extraordinary. The excitement, uncertainty – like a game. Dana used to take me to Wall Street with him. There's an incredible sort of fellow-feeling there, just like the war.'

'Dana advised you on money matters, did he?' Richard asked.

'Yes. He's become a director of Goldman Sachs, the big trading corporation. Right in the thick of it. I owe all my new-found wealth to his expertise.'

'Golly, James!' Georgina exclaimed. 'Are you really rich?' All three had been rather wondering this, in the light of the presents he had brought them, but delicacy had prevented their raising the subject.

'I'm not a millionaire,' he replied. 'But I'll pay for any scale of wedding you ask for. No, I insist. And Father . . . I've been thinking about this house. I might sell it for something larger. More convenient for you two and the children.'

Virginia touched his hand. 'It's a kind thought, James, but

the children are almost grown up. I don't think we need anywhere larger, do we darling?'

'Something smaller, if anything,' Richard agreed.

'All right, then. We'll have a villa in the South of France. Or a yacht.'

'You don't really mean it?' Georgina asked, agog.

'Of course I do. You don't seem to understand. It's open to everyone out there to make a small fortune. Everyone here, too, if they want it. Dana's chauffeur overheard a conversation in the back of the car, put all his life savings into Bethlehem Steel, and was able to retire overnight.'

Virginia was frowning. 'It somehow doesn't seem right to me,' she said.

'Why not? Why should it be regarded as immoral to make money? We work all our lives looking for prosperity, and when it comes it's treated as something vulgar. O.K., then. I stand rebuked, but unrepentant.'

'There's no question of rebuke,' Richard hastened to say, noting the ominous pink flush which had suffused his son's cheeks. 'Just a note of caution. One hears rumours . . .'

James laughed. 'Wall Street thrives on rumour. Anyway, money doesn't have to corrupt. So, will anyone join me in a toast to my investments . . . coupled with Georgina's wedding? May they both bring happiness to us all.'

'I'll join you,' Georgina said enthusiastically; and they all raised their glasses and drank.

Hudson and Daisy had been in attendance during the meal. Afterwards, for once, Daisy couldn't prevent herself alluding to a topic overhead.

'How do you make money on the Stock Exchange, Mr Hudson?'

He frowned his disapproval of her breaching the taboo, but decided that the question, being general and not personal, might be answered.

'You buy shares in companies dealing in certain commodities, Daisy. When the shares rise in value, you sell them and keep the profits. That's the simple principle.'

'Sounds easy. Can anyone do it?'

'Yes. But, you see, the shares can lose their value. Then when you sell them you're out of pocket. It's a matter of great expertise, judging which and when to buy and sell.'

Rose had been listening in. She said, 'But you have people to advise you, don't you? People who know about it.'

'Yes, Rose. You also have people advising you on horse racing, and look where they can land you. Speculation is just another word for gambling.'

'I wouldn't call the Major the gambling type.'

'That's different,' Mrs Bridges contributed her part to the discussion. 'The Major's a gentleman.'

'Quite right, Mrs Bridges,' Hudson said. 'The Stock Exchange is not for the likes of us.'

But a sudden madness had struck Rose. It grew on her overnight, resulting in many wakeful hours and, at length, a decision. Next morning she made a point of looking for something in the morning-room at a time when she knew James to be there.

'Hello, Rose,' he said. 'Where is everybody?'

'His lordship went out early, sir, and her ladyship just after breakfast.'

'Hm. And how have things been with you, Rose?'

'Much the same as usual, sir, thanks.'

'That's fine.'

'You're looking very well, sir.'

'I'm O.K.'

'Er . . . sir . . . could I talk to you for a minute, if you're not too busy?'

'Sure. Go ahead.'

'Well, I don't know if you remember, sir, but I was left some money by Sergeant Wilmot. It's in deposit in the bank, but I was wondering if I ought to invest some of it. You know, on the Stock Exchange.'

'That sounds like a good idea, Rose. Make more for you than lying in a bank.'

'I don't mean a lot of it, sir. Only a small amount.'

'The more you put in, the more you make. It's as simple as that.'

Rose hesitated. 'Hudson was talking about the Stock Exchange as if it was like gambling on horses.'

'Nothing of the sort. There's a world of difference between gambling and speculating. Your investments will help to build new factories, make new jobs for thousands of people. The bigger your company gets, the more profits it makes for you.'

She brightened. 'I hadn't thought of it like that. The trouble is knowing how much I should invest, and what to do?'

'I can see to it for you if you want me to, Rose. As to the amount, it's up to you.'

'I've got twelve hundred and seventy-five pounds altogether, but . . .'

'That's very good. But you must decide. It's your money.'

'I . . . I'd sooner leave it to you, sir.'

'All right, then. We'll put it all through an investment trust. That's like a bank, really, except that there are expert people to decide what to buy on your behalf and then keep selling and buying to your advantage.'

'That'd be fine, sir. I'm ever so grateful.'

'Not a bit. Well, there's no time like the present. What's this bank of yours?'

She told him, and by that afternoon the formalities had been completed. This little flurry of activity over, James found himself at a loose end. Looking round his own room, he suddenly decided that it depressed him with its sameness from so many years. He determined to clear it out and have it redecorated.

'I'll help,' Georgina said, equally glad of the prospect of activity.

'Thanks. It'll keep you out of mischief. I'm sure young Stockbridge would be glad of that. When's he coming back, anyway?'

'One hundred and sixty-five days.'

'Right. For one hundred and sixty-five days you're in my charge. We'll start tomorrow. Ride before breakfast. Downstairs in the hall sharp. O.K.?'

'O.K.'

After the ride and breakfast they started work on his room, beginning to clear the wardrobe and drawers. They had not been long at it when Edward came in with a letter on a salver. Seeing foreign stamps, Georgina hoped it was for her from Robert, but Edward proffered it to James.

'You still collect stamps, Edward?' James asked, tearing open the envelope carefully.

'Yes, sir.'

'There's a couple of George Washingtons for you, then.'

He handed over the envelope. Edward thanked him and went. James unfolded the notepaper unhurriedly and glanced at it. Georgina had turned her back to him, so did not see the sudden and dramatic change in his expression.

'I have to go out,' she heard him say, and the strain in his voice made her turn to him curiously. He was distinctly pale.

'What's the matter?'

'It's . . . nothing. But I must go out. I'm sorry.'

And he hurried from the room, leaving her to look helplessly at the disarray and then shrug her shoulders and go on adding to it.

Below stairs, the servants gathered round Mr Hudson who held an early edition of one of the evening newspapers. His ejaculation, 'Terrible news!' had drawn them away from their various tasks.

'What's happened?' Mrs Bridges asked, fearing a royal death or a railway disaster. His reply puzzled her.

'The slide has begun in earnest, I'm afraid.'

'Slide? What slide?'

'The economic slide in America. On Wall Street. The bottom has fallen out of the stock market.'

Rose's head jerked up sharply at this news. No one noticed. She had said nothing to them of her venture. She listened with growing concern to Mr Hudson's précis of the rest of the report.

'There have been signs of it for several days now. Rumours

circulating that shares have lost their value. Investors panicking and trying to sell, causing the shares to drop further in value. They're finally not worth the paper they're written on. Thousands have been ruined.'

'You see what I was telling you the other day,' he addressed Daisy. 'Exactly like placing money on horses.'

Rose risked saying, 'Anyway, it's lucky it's America and not here, isn't it?'

The butler shook his head gravely. 'Not at all, Rose. These affairs of high finance are international. Mark my words, the London Stock Exchange will react very badly to this.'

'You don't mean . . .' said Daisy, who had been thinking over his earlier words; '. . . you don't mean the Major's lost his money?'

Forgetting that only he and she had overheard the conversation in the dining-room actually alluding to the Major's newly-won wealth, and that he had ordered her to say nothing to the other servants about it, Hudson answered, 'Short of a miracle, I fear that may be so.'

Rose tried desperately to see James. She encountered him in the hall, just coming back into the house.

'Major James, sir . . .'

But he shook his head, hurrying towards the morning-room.

'Not just now, Rose.'

He went in, closing the door on her.

Richard, Virginia and Georgina were there with their copies of all the evening newspapers. James went straight to the drinks tray and poured himself a whisky. He drank it down and poured another.

'Put us out of our misery, James,' Georgina said.

'How badly has it hit you?' Virginia asked.

He banged the glass down hard. 'If Dana had only cabled instead of written I might have had time to do something. As it is, yes, I've been hit pretty hard.'

'Wiped out?'

'I don't know . . . Yes, I think so.'

Richard asked, 'Couldn't your London broker have warned you?'

'It happened too fast. First hint of real trouble was last Thursday, but the bankers stepped in and checked it. Yesterday, when the news was bad again, everyone thought they'd do the same, only they didn't. Goldman Sachs was buying its own stock, swindling itself to get confidence back. It was too late. Out of touch over here, that's the trouble. Lack of proper information. Snowball. Panic.'

He drained his glass and filled it again.

'We can sell my necklace,' Virginia volunteered.

'Yes,' Georgina added. 'And my fur.'

James shook his head numbly. 'No! Drops in the ocean, anyway. I borrowed a fair bit.'

'What about Elizabeth and Dana?'

'I shouldn't worry about them, Father. They'll have salvaged something.' He remembered something. 'There are other people to worry about than them.'

He sent for Rose to his own room. It was a summons she had been hoping for, yet fearing. She sensed the worst from his serious face and the invitation to her to sit on his green, buttoned leather settee.

'I'm not sure how much you know, Rose,' he began. There was no need to say about what.

'Hudson's explained some of it, sir, but I don't quite understand . . .'

'No. You see, certain things have happened on the American stock market which were unfortunately . . . outside our control. I'm afraid that my own investments . . . and the money you put in, too . . . well, they've both been lost.'

'You mean . . . all of it, sir? There's nothing left?'

'Nothing worth talking about. I'm sorry, Rose. I don't know what to say to you. I know how you must be feeling.'

She was feeling nothing. Strangely nothing.

'It wasn't your fault, I'm sure,' she said remotely. 'Never did mean much to me, anyway – money.'

He himself was aware of some relief.

'It's good of you to take it like that, Rose. It helps me feel better. And you must understand that we'll always look after you. You'll never want for anything. I give you my word on that.'

She got to her feet.

'Yes, I know that,' she said. 'Thank you, sir.'

Like an automaton, she left the room and went down to the servants' hall. There was no point in holding back from the others now. Her appearance showed them all that she had suffered some blow, and she was only grateful that Mr Hudson and Mrs Bridges shooed the junior servants away before persuading her to unburden herself.

'I . . . I don't know what to say, Rose,' Hudson stammered, trying not to sound harsh but unable to keep the note of censure out of his tone. 'Didn't I warn you? Did you not listen to what I said?'

'You said the stock market was for gentlemen, Mr Hudson. Well, the Major's a gentleman. He's supposed to know about money.'

'You didn't give him it all?' demanded Mrs Bridges, horrified at the sudden thought.

'Yes. I only wanted to do a little, but he said the more I put in, the more I'd make, and there wasn't any risk.'

'How could he do it?' Mrs Bridges demanded of Hudson. 'Risking a servant's money like that!'

'The Major's always had a rash streak in his nature, but I agree, this takes the biscuit.'

Rose was saying, 'What would Gregory have said, that's what I want to know? It was his money. I was, like, keeping it for him.'

'Now, now, dear . . .'

'Yes, Rose, calm yourself. It's not the end of your life. You still have us to look after you . . .'

She turned on him angrily.

'I don't want you to look after me. I want to look after myself, and I can't now. I'm stuck here for the rest of my rotten days, and Gregory'll never forgive me.'

She ran from the servants' hall. If Mr Hudson had been in her path to the door she would probably have pushed him out of the way.

The news inevitably reached Richard and Virginia. James had said nothing and Hudson, in consultation with Mrs Bridges, decided that no word should be allowed to leak from below stairs. Rose, too, had decided to say nothing, but some chance remark of Virginia's undermined her resolution and she broke down. She was gently persuaded to tell all.

When Virginia told Richard he reacted with shocked astonishment.

'James invested her money! What the devil did he think he was doing?'

'We must do something to make it up to her,' Virginia said. 'I'll stump up, but it can't be much.'

'I want to see him at once,' Richard said. She had never seen him so tense with anger as he rang the bell.

'Not now, Richard,' she requested. 'It's nearly lunch.'

'Damn lunch!'

Hudson was sent to fetch James to the morning-room. His father commenced savaging him as soon as the door was shut.

'I know you've lost a lot of money, but I never thought you'd stoop to borrowing from servants.'

'I did not borrow money. She came and asked me to invest it for her. Of her own free will. What was I supposed to do? Turn her away?'

'Of course you should have. Have you no sense? It's an absolutely unshakable rule that one never meddles with a servant's money.'

'I did not meddle with it. I invested it soundly. Anyway, it's not some private club for gentlemen only to become rich.'

'If she had "become rich", what then? How would a girl like Rose know what to do with wealth? You'd have given her ideas, dreams, responsibilities she couldn't have lived with.'

'What arrogance! She's not some half-wit family retainer. She's an intelligent woman. She knew the risk.'

'How? Did you tell her? Or did you say it was all easy? Did

she trust you as she's always trusted us? Either way, you've ruined her life and now what's to become of her? You can't afford to pay her back.'

James gestured helplessly and Virginia felt deep pity for him. He had acted foolishly, she could agree, but only in an attempt to help someone else. That he had failed had been a cruelly unlucky coincidence of timing. And to suggest that he had 'borrowed' the money, or that he had deluded an innocent with grandiose promises, struck her as downright unfair.

He mumbled, 'I'll do what I can for her. Not just at the moment, but as soon as I can.'

But Richard was unrelenting. 'You're wiped out, boy. What can you do? I just thank God your mother was spared this.'

'Mother?'

'She wouldn't have believed it of you. It would have broken her heart.'

'Mother lived in a different age, Father. We've moved on. There's been a war . . .'

'Oh, don't use the war as an excuse again. Anyway, we fought the war to keep your mother's world, to preserve certain standards of decent behaviour.'

Virginia saw James's control snap as he told his father, 'Now you're talking like an old fool!'

'What? How dare you . . .!'

'If you believe . . . Oh, it's hopeless even trying.'

'Hopeless. Yes, hopeless. That's the word for it exactly.'

'What do you mean?'

'I mean you, boy. Everything you do. Everything you turn to. Why – can you tell me – why, with all your advantages, it always ends the same? So much you could have done with your life, in whatever field you'd chosen. That by-election . . . You had a flair for politics, but no, you didn't stick with it . . .'

'Politics! You discouraged me, Father, right from the start. Now don't deny it. So what else was there? Back to commerce? Or stockbroking? Yes, that was possible – so long, I suppose, as I didn't throw any tips to poor servants and kept them strictly for us.'

'James . . .' Virginia said urgently, but neither man heard her. They were standing face to face, like fighters, swinging verbal blows at one another. Virginia was becoming frightened.

'Go on, what else?' James was demanding. 'The Colonial Service? Endless parties in damnable climates. Yes, that would have kept me out of trouble. Or after Hazel I could have found a nice, rich widow and become a gentleman of means and leisure. Would that have pleased you?'

'Yes, you could have married again. It would have given you responsibility, happiness . . .'

'Made me less selfish, you mean?'

'Frankly, yes. Children . . .'

'Are children so important to a man's happiness? Judging by this conversation, I'd have thought not. Anyway, if you remember, Hazel miscarried.'

Richard relented a little at this.

'Yes, yes, I know,' he said unaggressively. 'That was sad. But there's still time, James. It's up to you. I can't tell you what to do. All I can offer is my support and . . . and love. The love of the whole family. We're all behind you.'

'Love? Or pity?'

'Damn it, not pity!'

'I'm an embarrassment, aren't I? An awkward reminder of failure. Your failure, perhaps. Your disappointment.'

'Don't be absurd.'

'It's there in everything you say. Your friends confirm it every day, I expect. "How's James? Still drifting? Time he settled down and gave you a grandson or two to carry on the Bellamy line." '

'That's *self*-pity. Cynical, defeatist talk, and I can't bear to listen to it.'

'You started it . . .'

'*You* insisted on it. I merely wanted to arouse some pride in you. Some guts. To help you.'

'Help? You accuse me of some kind of immoral act with Rose. You attack my character on all fronts. Help! You haven't begun to understand what I am. I don't need you to tell me.'

Virginia's sympathy sprang to Richard now, as she saw how this had hurt. He almost pleaded, 'James, my dear boy . . .'

James shook his head. 'No. No conciliations now. That's how we always end up – patching the wounds. Let's leave them open this time.'

He strode to the door, wrenched it open, and went out, slamming it behind him. Richard stared after him, half-stunned. Virginia moved to his side.

The door opened again and Georgina came in, looking alarmed.

'What's the matter with James? What's been going on?'

They didn't answer. She ran out again, calling after James. She ran up the stairs and as she neared his door a blast of Wagner came from behind it. Although she knocked and called repeatedly and tried the handle, he would not let her in. The music crashed on, in reflection of his mood.

'Daisy – where's Rose?' Mr Hudson asked after the delayed luncheon had been served and the servants were about to sit down to their own.

'Dunno, Mr Hudson,' she replied. 'I saw her with her hat and coat on. Didn't say where she was going.'

'Gone out!'

'For a little walk, I expect,' Mrs Bridges said, dishing up. 'Settle herself down a bit.'

'She's no right to go for a walk without permission.'

'Oh, Mr Hudson, I think we have to be a bit more understanding, in view of what's happened.'

'I was quite prepared to be understanding, Mrs Bridges. But you heard what she said to me, as if I were to blame for the mess she's in. All that talk of independence . . . I've heard that before and it makes no impression on me. She's been free to leave this house these past ten years if she wanted to. She's always chosen to stay.'

Daisy said, 'She told me it's Gregory she feels she's lost.'

'Gregory? She lost him years ago.'

'Daisy's right,' Mrs Bridges said. 'So long as Rose had the

money she still had her Gregory. Now she's lost it, she's got nobody and nothing.'

He looked baffled. 'It's quite beyond me what the two of you are driving it.'

'That's because you're a man. It's hard for a man to understand these things.'

In the morning-room, Virginia was finding it equally hard to get Richard to understand.

'Why did you tell him he's a failure? It's the oldest thing in the world for a father to attack his son for not living up to expectations. You two are past masters at that sort of fight.'

'You're blaming me for what happened, then?'

'Yes, you must take some of the blame.'

'Damn it, someone's got to drive the boy. He seems totally unable to do it for himself.'

'He's perfectly able, if you'd only leave him alone. He was fine when he got back from America. Masses of energy.'

'But the wrong kind, my dear. Too volatile. Too highly strung. Too obsessed with the glamour of money. And now he's lost it all. I repeat, I meant simply to rap him over the knuckles, and suddenly we were laying his whole life out for examination.'

To his surprise, she was almost crying.

'Richard,' she said, with a kind of desperation, 'I think we must leave this house. Or James must. The two of you are impossible under the same roof. You bicker and fight. You upset everyone, including the servants. I won't stand for it. I can't do with it!'

'Virginia . . .' he began, but broke off as Hudson came in to take away the coffee tray.

Virginia blew her nose and asked, 'Hudson, do you know where Rose is? I was looking for her.'

'I believe she went out, m'lady. Without permission, I'm afraid. She was rather upset after the Major explained to her . . . Mrs Bridges and I did our best to console her, but . . .'

'I'm sure you did. Let me know the moment she comes in, will you?'

'Yes, m'lady. Would the Major like anything to eat? A tray in his room?'

'I expect he'll call if he wants anything.'

'Very good, m'lady.'

Georgina gained access to James's room at last. It was later that afternoon and the storm of music had ceased some time ago. She found him composed again as he added to the piles of objects taken from his various drawers.

'Come back to help?' he greeted her, and she joined in willingly.

One little pile, she noted, was entirely made up of wartime relics – a field compass, a telescope in a short leather case, a bayonet in a scabbard. He saw her looking at it.

'Edward can take that lot out to the rag-and-bone man for a start,' he said.

Georgina had wondered whether to steer clear of what had evidently been a painful scene in the morning-room, but curiosity and a desire to help and comfort James overcame her discretion. She asked, 'James, were you and Uncle Richard having one of your rows? What was it about?'

'Ask Father.'

'I'm asking you. Come on, Jumbo, don't keep it all bottled up.'

He turned to her. 'One thing I won't forgive him for – using Mother against me.'

'Your Mother? How?'

'Didn't he know? Didn't he know that coming back on that damned boat, all the time, I was staring down at that damned ocean, knowing she was down there somewhere?'

'Oh . . . James!'

'And he used her memory as a weapon against me.'

'He didn't mean it. He loved her, too. You mustn't hold it against him. Think of the future now. Don't keep looking back.'

He said wearily, 'Yes, you're right. I'm sorry. Here – photo of you and Hazel. You want it?'

'Don't you?'

'Take it, and all the rest of them. Make a scrapbook out of

them for your children. I don't want them.'

'Please don't be bitter.'

'I'm not.'

'I know you're unhappy. I know things are difficult. You've lost all that money and you're worried about . . .'

'The money's nothing, Georgina, believe me. I've only one regret about it, and that's that I can't give you the wedding I promised.'

'It doesn't matter.'

'It matters to me.'

'You'll still be there. You'll be the most important person, you know that.'

'What are you talking about? Your husband will be the most important person. I'll be of no use whatsoever.'

Another of his wounds had been rent open. He flung a pile of letters on to the rug in front of the burning fire. She recognised them at once.

'Those are my letters to you. From France,' she said.

'I know. I'm going to burn them. Did you keep mine?'

'I . . . They're somewhere, yes.'

'Fetch them. We'll make a pile of them and burn them together.'

'No!'

'Of course we must. You don't want your husband to find them by accident, do you?'

But Georgina had scooped up the pile of envelopes and was holding them protectively. He tried to snatch them from her and they struggled slightly over them.

'I don't want them burnt, James! They're mine. They're memories. They're nothing to be ashamed of, and I want them kept.'

He was too strong for her. With his mouth set cruelly, he gave the letters a vicious twist out of her hands and flung them on to the flames. Almost hysterically he snatched up others from a table top and flung them on, too. One fluttered to the rug. Georgina swiftly retrieved it, glanced at it, then looked at him horrified.

'This is from Hazel!'

'Yes!' he cried, seizing it and flinging it into the grate. 'And these are Mother's. They're all going. The whole bloody lot!'

The scene was too painful for her. She went sadly from the room and to her own. After a few minutes' brooding, she pulled herself together and sat down to write her daily letter to Robert. Within moments, James and his troubles were out of her mind.

An hour later, Virginia, crossing the hall, was surprised to see James coming downstairs in his hat and coat and carrying a valise.

'James . . . ?' she began, but he explained, 'I'm sorry I won't be in to dinner, Virginia. I've decided it's best if I go away for a few days. Give things time to cool off.'

'Where are you going?'

'An old army friend, Charles Stapleton, and his wife, in the country. They've often asked me.'

'James, your father's bitterly regretting what happened. We've been talking about it so much, and he says he didn't mean half of what he said. He's in his bath now, but won't you wait and talk to him before you go?'

'It'd be too soon. Some of the same things would be bound to be said. Just . . . tell him not to blame himself. He didn't say anything I didn't know already. Will you say goodbye for me?'

'Perhaps you're right. Yes.'

'Goodbye, Virginia.'

She looked sadly after him as he went through the front door. She longed to see him reconciled with his father and settled into some satisfying routine of life, but neither thing seemed possible to attain. Virginia sighed and went on into the morning-room.

It was after eleven o'clock that night, and Rose had still not returned. Edward and Daisy had retired to their flat over the garage and Ruby had long since gone up to her room. Mr Hudson and Mrs Bridges kept yawning vigil in the servants' hall. For the umpteenth time he looked at his watch and snapped it shut again.

'I must lock up soon,' he said.

'You can't, Angus. You can't shut the poor girl out. If you like, I'll wait up for her myself.'

'No, no. But if she's not back by midnight I feel I must inform her ladyship.'

'But they've gone to bed.'

'She is very anxious for news. I'm sure she would wish to be told.'

At that moment the front door bell rang. They looked at one another.

'She wouldn't come to the front door. Oh, Mr Hudson, I hope it isn't some bad news about the poor girl!'

Frowning worriedly, he slipped on his jacket and went up. He had no sooner disappeared from sight than the area door opened and Rose came in. She was drooping wearily.

'Rose! Wherever have you been all this time?' Mrs Bridges cried, more relieved than annoyed. 'Oh, we've been so worried, you naughty girl. Thank God nothing's happened to you.'

Rose sank into a chair, not removing her coat or hat.

'I took a bus ride,' she said in a flat tone. 'Number 25, Victoria to Ilford. My old route. I went and sat in the garage canteen. The old woman behind the counter remembered me. Then I got the last bus home.'

'And now you feel better, do you, dear?'

'Yeh. Funny, really, isn't it? None of it seems important any more. I'm just sorry I caused such a nuisance.'

'That's all right, dear,' Mrs Bridges smiled, patting her shoulder. 'I understand and so will Mr Hudson when I explain it to him. You get off to bed now. You must be tired out. Everything'll be all right in the morning, you'll see.'

Rose nodded and forced herself to her feet. They both turned towards the short staircase – and saw Hudson standing at the foot of it, ashen-faced.

The burly, grey-haired man who had introduced himself at

the front door as Chief-Inspector Rodwell and had insisted on Lord Bellamy's being roused, enlarged upon his doom-laden announcement to Richard and Virginia, who had come down together in their dressing-gowns.

'He was found two hours ago in a hotel room in Maidenhead. A chambermaid heard the shot and went to his aid, but he was dead within minutes. I can assure your lordship and your ladyship that he can't have suffered.'

'Shot?' mumbled the stricken Richard, who had been asleep when Hudson had called him and couldn't believe that he wasn't dreaming still. 'James – shot?'

'He appears to have shot himself through the roof of the mouth with a Service revolver, my lord.'

'Oh, God!' Virginia cried, and subsided onto the settee.

The inspector was holding out a white envelope towards Richard.

'He left this letter addressed to you. Also two others – for the coroner and for Sir Geoffrey Dillon, his solicitor.'

He fingered his bowler hat. 'I won't trouble you further tonight, my lord. We'll call back in the morning and see to the formalities, then. My, er, sincere condolences.'

He saw himself out. For a few moments Richard stood motionless. The stranger's absence made the situation feel even more unreal, as though it had never happened. But when he looked down he saw the envelope still in his hand. He crumpled onto the settee beside Virginia, who clutched him and nursed him like a child.

It was many minutes before they could bring themselves to open the envelope and read the letter:

Dear Father,

Do you remember me telling you about that German officer in the shell crater at Passchendaele who should have finished me off but declined to? Well, I'm doing the job for him. It's nothing to do with our talk today. Mother always said to leave when you're winning is not ethical, and we both know my losing streak has been going on far too long.

Try and see it as a soldier's way out when he can no longer do justice to himself or the men under his command. I choose this place so as not to make a mess of my room or inconvenience anyone more than is necessary. I've sent my will to Sir Geoffrey (unwitnessed I'm afraid, but I'm sure he will manage). Goodbye, Father. Give my love to Virginia and to Georgina. Don't be sad.

James

CHAPTER EIGHT

James's suicide did more than end his life and plunge his family into grief and their servants into shocked dismay: it precipitated the disintegration of the household enclosed within the walls of No. 165 Eaton Place.

Sir Geoffrey Dillon, spelt out the implications of it to Richard, Virginia and Georgina in their morning-room one early summer morning of 1930. The months which had elapsed since the tragedy had, as the passage of time usually will, served to diminish the pain and sorrow, but had conversely deepened everyone's concern for what the future held in store. Now the calculations had been made and Sir Geoffrey's habitually dour countenance showed no special sign of reassurance for the occasion.

'I'm afraid the final report doesn't make very pleasant reading,' he said, shuffling papers. 'You, Miss Worsley, as the principal legatee of Major Bellamy's estate, are the person most concerned. But, to put it in blunt lay terms, I'm afraid there won't be any estate left to inherit.'

It was Richard who questioned him. 'You mean, there are no . . . ?'

'Assets? No. Rather the reverse. Unfortunately, James incurred a great many debts in the last few months of his life. In addition, he was very generous in loans to his friends.'

'He thought he was rich,' Virginia pointed out. 'He was, for a time. How could he guess the crash was coming? I mean, no one else did.'

'I am not trying to allocate blame, Lady Bellamy. I'm just explaining the facts, as is my duty as executor of your stepson's estate.'

Georgina asked anxiously, 'Sir Geoffrey, it won't mean that I'm liable for . . . for his debts?'

'No, no. Oh, no, no.'

Richard asked, 'You have taken into account the sale of the remainder of the lease of this house? I mean to say, we've been expecting that it will have to be sold.'

'It will indeed have to be sold. As you know, however, it was James's property and the proceeds must be set against his liabilities. I have already made some enquiries about the best method of selling. The property market isn't exactly buoyant at this moment, but happily there is still some interest in houses in Belgravia such as this one – for redevelopment.'

'You mean . . . they'll pull it down?'

'Oh, no. Convert it into flats. Modernise generally. I mean, nowadays, when nobody can afford servants any more . . .'

He lapsed into a tactful fit of coughing as he saw Hudson and Daisy come through the door with coffee things. Virginia could perceive from Daisy's eyes that she, at least, had overheard the last few words. She told them to leave the tray for her to manage. Hudson put it on a low table beside her and the servants retired.

Sir Geoffrey resumed. 'There's a question of fixing a date for the auction . . .'

'Auction?' Richard echoed. 'I thought an agent would deal with it.'

'Of the contents, I mean.'

Virginia looked up from pouring coffee. 'But won't Georgina even get the furniture?'

'I'm afraid not. Everything will need to be sold to help pay the debts. By the way, I would be glad if you would make a list of those goods and chattels you believe to be your personal possessions.'

Virginia saw the shaking of Georgina's hand as she accepted her coffee cup. She recognised that the girl was struggling to hold back tears. The suicide of the only man she had really loved apart from Robert had hit her harder than any of them. Her pity for James had been profound and she had been tormenting herself with the thought that if she had only accepted his most recent proposal to marry her he would have been alive still and perhaps happy and fulfilled at last. This speculation was fuelled by the continued absence of Robert, who had been abroad for some weeks longer than the bargained-for period. She had found it difficult to write to him since James's death. Although he was now en route for home at last, she felt that he and she were drifting apart, rather than coming closer. Depression and a loss of any confidence in the future seemed to be weighing more heavily upon her each day.

Virginia asked, 'Sir Geoffrey, is there anything you want Georgina to sign?'

'No. Not at present.'

'Then may she be excused?'

He raised his eyebrows in uncomprehending surprise at the request.

'Certainly. Of course.'

Georgina went quickly and thankfully, just managing to preserve her self-control as far as her room, where she lay on her bed and cried.

Richard explained to the lawyer, 'The poor girl's rather upset still, I'm afraid.'

'Quite. Now, about a convenient date for the auction? And, indeed, for vacant possession of the premises.'

'This has all come at a difficult time for us, you see, Geoffrey,' said Richard. 'It rather depends if and when Georgina gets married. To Robert Stockbridge, you know.'

'Ah, yes. But I rather thought that had fallen through.'

'There's no reason to presume that. He's due back any day now, and then they have to decide.'

'If I know the Duchess of Buckminster,' Sir Geoffrey said bleakly, 'she'll be the one who decides.'

'It was more or less an unspoken agreement that if they still wish to marry after this separation, they may.'

'Mm.'

Virginia said, 'So if we could have just a little longer before making any decisions? It would be so much more convenient if she could be married from here.'

Sir Geoffrey replaced the papers in his case and snapped it shut as he rose.

'Very well, then. At your earliest convenience.'

Virginia went up to Georgina as soon as the lawyer had gone. She found her dry-eyed but sounding deeply pessimistic.

'I haven't had a letter for seventeen days.'

'But if he's on the ship I don't expect he can write.'

'It calls at different places all the time. Aden and Port Said and Malta . . .'

'I don't imagine the post is too good from those sort of places. If . . . if anything drastic had happened . . . If he'd . . . changed his mind, I'm sure he would have let you know by cable or something.'

Georgina shook her head. 'Knowing Robert, I think he'd want to . . . to tell me to my face.'

Virginia smiled and patted her. 'I'm sure he'll want to tell you to your face that he still loves you. Where does the ship arrive?'

'Plymouth first. Then it comes on to London.'

'Shall you go to meet it?'

Georgina thought for a few moments.

'I think I'd better not,' she said at length.

In yet another contravention of the rules about reporting conversation overheard above stairs, Mr Hudson had had no compunction in confiding in Mrs Bridges; and Daisy had told Eddie, who had agreed with her that, if there was going to be a bust-up, it was only fair and proper that Rose and Ruby should know, too.

'Well, it didn't come exactly as a surprise, did it?' was Rose's reaction. She, more than any of them, had been in the forefront of the preceding events.

Edward looked up from the newspaper. 'Not a thing in *Situations Vacant*. Columns of *Situations Wanted*.'

'No wonder, with over two million unemployed,' Mr Hudson answered. 'What we want is a man like this Mussolini. Anyone out of work in Italy he puts on to making roads and railway stations.'

'I don't want to make roads and railway stations! What I want to know is, where's all the money gone to? I mean, one minute everyone's rich – lots of gold, money in the bank, shares and all that. Next minute they're all skint. I mean, gold doesn't vanish into thin air!'

Mr Hudson was for once on the side of unreason, making none of his usual efforts to rationalise things for his inferiors.

'It's all the government's fault,' he said. 'They never should have got rid of Mr Baldwin. Though I say it myself, Ramsay MacDonald's a disgrace to Scotland. But then, I've heard tell the MacDonalds weren't too steady at Culloden, either.'

'Yeh. But it's all right for you, Mr Hudson,' Daisy said truculently. 'Not all of us have sisters leave us boarding-houses at Hastings.'

It was true. In one of those gestures which Fate seems to extend towards some people of opening a fresh door just as an old one seems about to close, Mr Hudson's sister Fiona had died. Her will had proved to be simplicity itself, as notified to him by her solicitor: she had left him the going concern of the last of her succession of establishments, 'Seaview', Cambridge Road, Hastings. Pausing briefly to consider what his reaction to this would have been had his future at Eaton Place been secure, he had made up his mind and called Mrs Bridges into his pantry for a long discussion, from which they had emerged partners in the new venture of running 'Seaview'; he as proprietor and dining-room manager, she as cook and housekeeper.

'Guest-house, Daisy,' he corrected her use of the term 'boarding-house'. 'Our aim will be to attract the children of the better class . . . and, of course, their nannies and governesses.'

' "Seaview",' Edward mused. 'Be able to watch all the ships, then.'

'It, er, doesn't actually overlook the sea. It is considered better not to be on the actual front, on account of the storms . . . and the noise of the traffic.'

'That's right,' said Mrs Bridges, entering. 'But from the top floor there's a lovely view of the cliffs, over the other housetops.'

Edward winked at Daisy. She was too concerned for their own future to be much amused.

'Look!' Ruby exclaimed, waving the old copy of the *Tatler* she was cutting up for her scrapbook. 'There's a picture here of the Marquis of Stockbridge dancing with the Lady Felicity Cairns at a ball. Ooh, she does look happy!'

Rose looked, and said contemptuously, 'At the Viceregal lodge in Delhi. That was weeks ago.'

'Nevertheless,' Mr Hudson reminded her, 'last year, Lady Felicity, who, by the way, is the daughter of the Earl of Leyburn, was considered one of the most eligible debutantes of the season.'

'Yeh,' said Rose. 'I wouldn't wonder if the Duke and Duchess of Buckminster hadn't remembered that.'

Ruby said, 'Poor Miss Georgina. I don't reckon she's got a 'ope.'

'Ruby, is the water boiling for those sprouts?' Mrs Bridges demanded. 'If it isn't, you'd better get it turned up, 'stead of sitting there talking about things that don't concern you.'

'Yes, Mrs Bridges.'

The much-tried cook rolled her eyes ceiling-ward. 'That girl! She wouldn't know Christmas from Easter!'

Next morning, Daisy took Georgina's breakfast up to her room. She found her mistress dressed and made-up, but sitting in front of the dressing-table mirror, staring at her reflection.

'I don't want anything,' she said. 'I look a hundred, don't I?'

'I'm sure everything will be all right, miss. You must try and eat a little . . .'

The sound of a taxi coming to a halt outside caused Georgina to leap up and rush to the window. Daisy heard her gasp, then stepped quickly aside, trying to keep the tray level, as Georgina ran past her out of the room.

Hudson opened the front door to Robert Stockbridge, leaner and fitter-looking, tanned by tropical suns, wearing a rumpled suit which gave evidence of hurried travel.

'Hello, Hudson. Nice to see you again.'

'Yes, indeed, m'lord. I trust you enjoyed . . .'

Lord Stockbridge's eyes were no longer on him. They were on the girl who had reached the bend of the stairs and paused there, holding her breath, uncertain whether to come down further.

'Darling!' he cried, running forward. 'My darling Georgina! It's all right!'

Hudson slipped discreetly away through the pass-door. Georgina came slowly down the remaining stairs, letting Robert take her in his arms and almost hanging there.

'It's all right,' she thought she heard him say again. 'I saw my parents yesterday, in Nice. They've given us their blessing.'

'Nice . . . ?' she murmured, overwhelmed.

'Yes. They're staying on the Riviera, so I nipped off the boat at Marseilles and came back on the train. They were really very decent. Father was pleased as Punch, but he didn't dare admit it, and Mother said it was never anything to do with you, but it was me who was the hopeless, catty, unreliable one.'

He steered her firmly into the morning-room, which was empty.

'It was all terribly silly, the whole thing. Mother deliberately throwing every suitable girl in my way from Gibraltar to San Francisco, but I didn't turn a hair. I passed my test with flying colours. And, darling, darling, I love you so much . . . Have you heard a word I've said?'

'Not . . . really,' she murmured dazedly. 'I've . . . spent so long telling myself it wouldn't happen . . . and now it has, I just . . .'

She swayed in his arms. He hastily guided her on to the settee.

'I'm sorry, darling,' she said. 'I hope I'm not going to be sick. I feel all giddy.'

'Are you ill? Have you seen a doctor?'

She shook her head. 'It's not that. It's just that . . . everything's been so awful.'

Robert sat beside her, holding her hands.

'Yes, I know it has. I nearly came back when . . . when it

happened; but then I thought it might ruin everything if I did. Mother could say I'd cheated. You poor things! What a ghastly time you've had.'

Georgina said, almost to herself, 'I didn't realise how much James meant to me. I thought I'd managed to get him out of myself long ago. I suppose our lives had been mixed up together for so long . . . just burning letters and throwing things away wasn't any good. When it happened, I knew just how much I loved him. Oh, darling, it's not how I love you – not a bit like that. It's something I can't actually explain. I just feel as if a whole bit of me was numb . . . not working. I . . . I really don't think I ought to marry you.'

Robert, who had looked increasingly unhappy during this, was now alarmed.

'Darling, that's just silly!' he protested.

She went on: 'What I really mean is that I don't think you should marry me. I'm the scatty, unreliable one. That's what your mother really thinks, and she's right. I oughtn't to marry anyone, let alone try to be a marchioness. I don't want to see anyone. I don't want to do anything . . . Anyway, I can't get married. I haven't any money. I can't even pay for my own wedding dress.'

'But that's absurd,' he argued anxiously, sensing approaching hysteria in her tone. 'We'll be married in a Registry Office. I don't care two hoots what people will think . . . We'll find a way. All that matters to me is that I love you and adore you, and want you for my wife.'

But again she seemed not to have been listening. She murmured, through welling tears, 'You see, James was going to give me my wedding – the best wedding there's ever been, he said. And he left me everything he had in his will . . . only, the awful thing is that he didn't have anything. He had nothing. Poor James! He had nothing at all!'

Before he could clutch her she had run from the room, weeping.

Robert, who had had very little sleep on the train and, besides, had burned up much energy in sheer nervous tension, sought out Virginia and had a brief and friendly, though anxious, interview with her. He reported what Georgina had told him of her doubts and fears, and especially of her seeming insistence that since James's wish to pay for her wedding could not now be fulfilled, and she could not afford it herself, no wedding could take place.

'I see now I should have sent a cable or something from France,' he said miserably. 'I wanted to give her a surprise. I suppose it was the wrong thing.'

'Don't blame yourself, Robert,' Virginia said. 'She's been in a turmoil ever since James killed himself. She absolutely refuses to see a doctor, though. She won't even take a holiday. It's like some sort of obsession. Oh, I'm so sorry you've come back to find it like this.'

Absence and enduring love had done much for Robert Stockbridge's spirit, however.

'I'm not going to give up now,' he assured Virginia. 'Not after waiting so long.'

That evening she was working out lists and estimates when Richard came into the morning-room, shaking his head. His first action was to pour himself a large whisky and soda.

'I am absolutely bamboozled by the whole thing,' he declared. He had just come from Georgina's room.

'How is she now?'

'Oh, perfectly calm. She says she's sorry to have caused us so much trouble – that she isn't sure she ever wanted to get married in the first place – that we're to go ahead with our plans for leaving this house as if she didn't exist . . . I really believe there may be something in that old wives' tale about a streak of madness in the Worsley family.'

'Nonsense. I understand exactly how she feels.'

'*You* understand?'

'Yes. Being a woman, too, I'm also a bit mad and illogical.'

'Well, if you'll kindly explain . . .'

'Oh, I couldn't possibly explain.'

Instead, she got up and kissed him, then drew him over to her desk.

'Darling, I want you to look at these estimates I've been making of the cost of the wedding. See if you agree.'

'But . . . but there isn't going to be . . .'

'As the Boy Scouts say, "Be prepared!" If she does decide to get married, we must pay for it.'

'That goes without saying. I'm her guardian. Somehow or other I must pay for it. But since she absolutely refuses . . .'

'I want to pay half. I've got some War Loans that should just about do it. No, don't look like that. If I want to stump up, I shall. Now, do have a look please.'

He did, and was astounded.

'Seven hundred and fifty guests! St Margaret's, Westminster! My dear Virginia, surely everyone will understand if it's a quiet wedding . . . the little church as Southwold, perhaps?'

'If it's to be done at all, it's to be done properly.'

'Ah, well, since it's only pure speculation anyway . . . "Choir and organist, seven pounds" . . . That's a bit steep, isn't it?'

'No. I've checked.'

' "Tip to verger, flowers in church, hired cars, printing and engraving . . . reception, thirty shillings a head"!'

'That's with a good champagne.'

He smiled, feeling now that he was entering into a joke with her.

'Quite right. Bad champagne at the reception is the worst start a marriage can have. Good Lord! "Trousseau and wedding dress, three hundred pounds". What on earth does it all add up to?'

'About seventeen hundred and fifty pounds.'

'Phew! I'm beginning to be quite glad it may never happen.'

'Just leave that to me, darling.'

He looked at her with deepest suspicion. She was smiling an enigmatic smile whose significance he had learned to respect.

A few days later, Mr Hudson showed Sir Geoffrey Dillon into the morning-room. Virginia received him. He refused sherry but accepted gin and bitters, of which, with her back to him, Virginia made a strong mixture.

'I have the lists of goods and chattels from your husband,' he said. 'Rather more comprehensive than I had expected, but I've no doubt I'll be able to get them past the creditors.'

'Good.'

'Now, as to the date of the sale . . .' he was getting out his diary. 'I presume that is what you wished to discuss with me, Lady Bellamy?'

'No. At least, not entirely. Sir Geoffrey, I know what a tower of strength to this family you've been over the years . . .'

He simpered a little. The strength of the gin was to his liking.

'. . . and I wanted to ask for your advice and help. It's about Georgina and her marriage.'

A request for help was always enough to put Sir Geoffrey Dillon on to his guard. He waited cautiously. Virginia went on, smiling winningly, leaning a little towards him in a conspiratorial way.

'It's a little delicate and highly confidential. I want you to write to Georgina, officially, saying you have discovered that when all was paid up there was still two thousand pounds left from James's estate.'

'But . . . but that's not true!'

'I know. Here is a cheque for two thousand pounds, made out to your firm.'

He looked at it in her hand as if to touch it would give him an electric shock.

'Are you asking me to . . . to enter into a conspiracy with you . . . To . . . to utter a lie in writing?'

'A little white lie isn't a crime, is it?'

'It's most unprofessional. If the Law Society were to hear . . .'

'They won't. Only you, and I and Richard will ever know.'

'And if the creditors heard of it they'd quite rightly want to know . . .'

'But they won't hear of it either.'

'Can you tell me the reason for this – this escapade?'

Virginia shook her head. 'I'm sorry, I can't. But I can assure you that we shall always be very grateful to you for your . . .'

(she had the right word ready) '. . . your courage. I am sure Georgina will remain your client, and of course, she will one day be a duchess.'

They looked at one another, long and hard. Then he sighed, reached out his hand, and without a word took the cheque. He locked it away in his case as swiftly as if it had been some creature likely to escape through his fingers.

Two mornings later Daisy brought in Georgina's breakfast on a tray. Georgina, still in bed, glanced at it with her usual distaste.

'Good morning, Daisy,' she said listlessly. 'How did you get on yesterday?'

Daisy's glumness matched her own.

'We went to two more agencies. They wouldn't even put us on their books when they heard we was married. It was like having leprosy.'

Georgina's gloom deepened even further. She languidly picked up the envelope lying on her tray and slit it open with her butter-knife. Daisy went on, 'They just said they was full up. Then we went to the Town Hall, and they said Edward would get seventeen bob a week on the dole, and I'd get nine. So we had a cup of tea and a bun and came home, miss. Edward's started talking about emigrating.'

Georgina said, 'I think I'll have to join you . . .' But she had by now unfolded the letter and taken in its brief, typewritten message.

'Daisy!' she cried.

Daisy, who had turned away to tidy Georgina's clothes, looked round, to see her face aglow and eyes wide.

'Daisy!' she repeated. 'Dressing-gown. Quick!'

The astonished maid provided the silk gown. Georgina was already out of bed and into her slippers. Flinging on the robe, she ran from the room.

'Uncle Richard!' she cried, bursting into the morning-room, where he and Virginia were examining some catalogues. 'Virginia! The most fabulously extraordinary thing's happened!'

She thrust the letter into Richard's hand. As soon as he

recognised the letter-heading of Dillon's firm he found it necessary to restrain himself from glancing up at Virginia.

'Two thousand pounds?' he managed to exclaim with convincing surprise. 'Darling, wonderful news. Georgina's going to inherit two thousand pounds from James's estate after all!'

Virginia was not to be outdone in acting. She made it easier for herself, though, by seizing Georginia in a great hug, so that it was over her shoulder, under the quizzical gaze of her husband, that she exclaimed in turn, 'Oh darling, how wonderful!'

Both Richard and Virginia knew inward relief when Georgina said what they had been almost praying she would: 'Do you think it would be terribly wickedly selfish and extravagant to spend it on getting married?'

'Of course not, darling,' Virginia told her.

Richard was able to say in all sincerity, 'That's what James would have wanted you to spend it on.'

From that moment Georgina was a changed person, to everyone's delight, not least Robert Stockbridge's. Her banished gloom and eager participation in the wedding preparations served to expunge the last of the grieving over James and restored optimism for what the future would have to offer each one of them.

Virginia remained in charge of the preparations, though. As the great day approached she sent for Mrs Bridges. The cook came into the morning-room with a wary air, as if expecting trouble.

'You wished to see me, m'lady?'

'Yes, Mrs Bridges. Sit down. It's about the wedding reception.'

Mrs Bridges sat with relief.

'As you know, it will be at Seaford House. Lord and Lady Howard de Walden have always been family friends.'

'Oh, I've often had the pleasure of cooking dinner for his lordship and her ladyship as guests.'

'Of course. It's sad we can't have it here, though, but there simply wouldn't be room. There will be caterers looking after the drinks and refreshments, but I was wondering . . . well, it was Miss Georgina's suggestion, really . . . I was wondering if you could undertake to make the cake?'

It was as well that Mrs Bridges was seated. Standing, she would perhaps have reeled, so great was the astonishment she showed.

'The wedding cake? Oh, lor' . . . Beg pardon, my lady. I mean, I should be delighted . . . and honoured. Of course, it would have to be some size, wouldn't it?'

'The bigger the better.'

'I've never done more than two tiers before, but I have seen four tiers. There was an illustration of one in the *News* when the Princess Royal married Lord Harewood.'

'Do you think you could manage four tiers, Mrs Bridges?'

'Well, I'll have a try. If I had to stop at three, I hope that would be acceptable?'

'Of course.'

'But I'll do my best for four, m'lady. It will be rather costly, though – all that marzipan.'

'Don't worry about that.'

'We'll have to hire a silver base, and I'll need a turntable for doing the decorating. But I can borrow one from my friend at Gunter's.'

'Splendid. No other problems?'

'No thank you, my lady.'

Mrs Bridges got stiffly to her feet.

'May I say again, m'lady, it's an honour and a pleasure.'

'Good luck, Mrs Bridges.'

Mrs Bridges was past the stage of being able to move quickly, but she made her way down to the kitchen with surprising energy. Ruby watched with open mouth as she selected a book which had remained unmoved from its place on the shelf for as long as Ruby could remember. Taking it to the table, Mrs Bridges began leafing through. Ruby moved closer and saw illustrations of wedding cakes of all sizes and designs.

'I haven't had this book out since Miss Elizabeth's wedding,'

Mrs Bridges said. She stopped turning the pages and pointed. 'There! That's the one I'll try – The Imperial.'

'We'll never manage that, Mrs Bridges!'

'Won't we, indeed? Listen to the ingredients: four pounds orange and lemon peel, eight pounds citron, sixteen pounds currants . . . Just think of that – *sixteen* pounds of currants. Ruby, just you get out all the baking pans we have in the house and start cleaning them. This instant!'

'Yes, Mrs Bridges.'

Through in the servants' hall, Rose and Mr Hudson looked up with – respectively – surprise and disapproval as Edward and Daisy came clattering down the short staircase together.

'Edward! Daisy . . . ! Mr Hudson began, but they ignored the reproof.

'They've asked us to work for them!'

'Who's "them"?' Rose asked.

'Lord Stockbridge and Miss Georgina. They just had us in and said they're going to move into a house on the estate at Shalford. If we wouldn't mind the country there's a nice little cottage for us.'

'Mind! We wouldn't mind an old tin shack, would we, Eddie?'

'He said he didn't want a chauffeur, as he likes driving himself. But they was looking for a sort of general manservant . . .'

'A butler, you mean?' Mr Hudson asked.

'He didn't say that exactly . . .'

'Then I think you should get it made very clear, Edward.'

'Well, beggars can't be choosers.'

'There is such a thing as dignity and respect.'

But they were in no mood for the niceties. Daisy bubbled, 'And Miss Georgina said she'd like me to be her personal maid, but that if I was . . . if we was to start a baby again, or anything, it would be quite all right. They'd always look after us.'

She burst into tears.

'Here, – Dais – what you crying for?' Edward asked, putting his arm round her.

'Oh, you wouldn't understand,' Rose told him. 'Honestly – men!'

Mrs Bridges set about the cake like an architect building a cathedral – except that no hands were allowed to touch the edifice besides her own. Ruby's function was strictly that of preparer and supplier, though with strict instructions not to come near the table more than was necessary.

'I've sieved the rest of the icing sugar, Mrs Bridges,' she ventured to say from a distance.

'Bring it here, then – *carefully*!'

Ruby laid down the basin on a corner of the table, amongst the litter of nozzles, syringe-like instruments and pieces of decoration.

'Now you can break four eggs and separate the whites.'

'Yes, Mrs Bridges.'

Mrs Bridges looked up at the cringing girl and softened a little.

'What are you going to do, Ruby?'

'Break four eggs and . . .'

'No, no! I mean with yourself? In the future?'

'I haven't really thought, Mrs Bridges.'

'Well, it's high time you did, then.'

'I might be an usherette in the cinema. You can see all the films free, twelve times a week.'

'Still got that Rudolph Valentino on the brain, have you?'

'Oh, no, he's gone a long time. It's talkies now.' Her eyes glazed. 'Ramon Novarro, Ronald Colman, John Barrymore . . . Oh, he's lovely, is John Barrymore.'

In her trance she had wandered dangerously close to the part of the table where the cake stood. Mrs Bridges shooed her away and resumed her concentration.

'May I suggest this tie, m'lord?'

Mr Hudson was valeting Richard as he dressed to go down to the House of Lords. Richard approved the choice.

'Yes – suitably sombre for my last speech from the front bench.'

'If I may say so, m'lord, it is a sad day for the Conservative Party, and for the nation.'

'Oh, nonsense. High time I made way for someone younger. Anyway, I'm looking forward to a quiet life in the country, writing my memoirs and just sitting back.'

'Your lordship will have a good deal to write about, I fancy. We have lived through some stirring times.'

'Yes. We've lived through a lot of history together, haven't we, Hudson?'

He put his arms into the morning coat Hudson was holding for him.

'I shall miss you very much, Hudson. You and Mrs Bridges. No one has been luckier with servants than we have. I only wish there was some more material way in which we could show our appreciation.'

'Oh, don't worry about that, m'lord, thank you. Mrs Bridges and I are well placed between us in that respect.'

Richard turned for Hudson to adjust his buttonhole and his eye fell on the open wardrobe with its long row of suits.

'Look at all those suits,' he said. 'You've never let me get rid of a suit, have you, Hudson? Some of them hardly worn, and I'll never need a quarter of them. If . . . if there are one or two that would be any use to you, you have only to say so.'

'Why, thank you, my lord. That is exceedingly kind of your lordship.'

Richard took his leave. When he had gone, Hudson went to the wardrobe and examined the suits with interest. One in particular took his eye. He took it out on its hanger and held it in front of himself before a mirror. The jacket was black and the trousers pepper-and-salt. The reflection in the glass was much to his liking.

When Virginia had kissed Richard and seen him driven off by Edward she went back into the morning-room where piles of correspondence – mostly acceptances to the wedding – awaited her. Rose came in and stood expectantly.

'Oh, Rose, I won't be able to go through those drawers with

you today, after all. Look – I'm completely snowed under with all this.'

Rose laughed. 'I can see that, m'lady.'

Virginia came to her. 'Rose, my dear,' she said, 'in all the huffle of Miss Georgina's wedding I haven't really found time to talk to you about your future, have I? I'm afraid his lordship and I have just rather taken it for granted that you'd be coming down to Dorset with us.'

She wasn't aware how relieved Rose was to hear this. She had been wondering why nothing had been said, and what that might portend.

Virginia went on, 'Of course, we'll be living a much more quiet and modest sort of life. We'll have to manage with fewer servants . . . just a cook and a girl from the village. So it's only fair to say that if you feel you would be happier elsewhere – staying in London, perhaps – then you're quite free . . .'

'Oh no, m'lady,' Rose interrupted hurriedly. 'Don't you worry. I'm quite a jack of all trades. I can turn my hand to most things about the house. All except cooking – I don't think I could boil an egg, even. But I'm country born and bred. I used to be a dab hand in the garden. When we was all in the village school at Southwold we each of us had a little garden of our own by the playground, and one year I won the prize, a new sixpence. I think I've still got it among . . .'

She broke off, suddenly realising how she had gabbled on in her relief. She added more slowly, 'I really am looking forward to going on looking after you and his lordship, and Miss Alice and Master William, my lady. Thank you . . . for letting me.'

Virginia smiled. 'You're one of the family anyway, Rose.'

The door opened. Georgina came in and held it ajar to enable Mr Hudson to pass in with a tray piled high with more letters.

'Oh, no!' Virginia groaned. 'Do you know, so far we've had three hundred and seventy-two acceptances and only thirty-one refusals?'

'Lor'!' Georgina exclaimed. 'We'll never fit them all into the church.'

Hudson and Rose left, each smiling for a different reason.

That evening, Richard and Virginia paid a state visit to the kitchen. Mr Hudson received them, smirking anticipatorily. Rose, Edward and Daisy were shuffling into line. Ruby was holding a chair, on the seat of which stood Mrs Bridges, putting the final touches to the most magnificent cake any of them had ever seen. It was four tiers tall.

'Oh, it's marvellous!' Virginia said.

'Superb!' Richard agreed. 'I really think someone should fetch Georgina down to see it.'

'Oh, no, m'lord,' Mrs Bridges said, as she was helped down. 'It would never do for a bride to see her cake before The Day.'

'I see. Well, congratulations, Mrs Bridges. I'm sure this is your masterpiece.'

'That, my lord, is what we have all been saying,' said Mr Hudson. He was positively beaming.

And so the wedding day came, and London society rejoiced. Georgina, wearing the Buckminster tiara – so precious that it had had to be brought to her by a policeman – was radiant. Robert was handsome and happy. The Duke and Duchess of Buckminster went out of their way to be friendly with Richard and Virginia and finished up being genuinely so. A chimney-sweep, just chancing to be passing as Georgina was about to enter the car, kissed her for luck, to loud cheers, and received a golden guinea which just chanced to be ready in one of Richard's waistcoat pockets. And when it was all over, photographs were taken, and champagne drunk, and speeches made, and more champagne drunk, and the great cake cut (loudest cheering of the day) . . . and the happy couple were driven off to the station, while the rest of the Eaton Place household returned – none of them entirely steady on their legs – to a house which had been visited in their absence by the estate agent's men and an auction notice hung on its railings.

This did little to depress their spirits, though, for there was a further celebration to come within less than twenty-four hours. Late the next morning, an incredulous Richard and Virginia turned towards the morning-room doors, to see Mr Hudson – who had asked for an appointment – usher Mrs

Bridges in and stand by her side. Richard noted that Hudson was wearing a dark jacket with pepper-and-salt trousers which he seemed to recognise.

'My lord, m'lady – if I might introduce Mrs *Hudson* to you?'

They gasped audibly. Then Richard stepped swiftly forward to shake his butler's hand, while Virginia gave her cook a great kiss.

'It has taken a wee while to get her to the altar, m'lady, but I've managed it at last,' Hudson explained, while Richard poured drinks for them all. 'However, we're just back from the Registry Office' – he produced the certificate – 'so she can't get away now.'

'The man was ever so nice, m'lady,' Mrs Bridges said, colouring up. 'He said in the eyes of the Lord it was better late than never.'

Richard insisted on their both sitting down to take their drink, then gave a toast to their happiness.

Hudson explained, 'We thought it best, m'lord, seeing that we are about to enter a new social circle in which our relationship might be misinterpreted.'

His wife nodded vigorously. 'They've got evil minds, some of them with nothing better to do at them small places by the sea. I remember in the war when I went down to visit my sister and brother-in-law at Yarmouth after that terrible bombing. There was a woman in the next street who'd been killed and found stone dead in bed with . . .'

Her husband placed his hand under her elbow and helped her to her feet.

'Yes, my dear, but that's rather a long story, isn't it? Now, if you'll excuse us, m'lord, m'lady, it is half-past twelve, and luncheon is at one.'

'Of course,' Virginia said. 'Congratulations again, both of you. And, by the way, if you would like some of the pots and pans and kitchen things to help stock your guest house, please be sure to let me know before the auctioneers come to make their inventory for the sale.'

'That is most kind of your ladyship.'

'And I hope you'll have an appropriate celebration tonight in the servants' hall – at my expense, of course,' Richard added.

'Thank *you*, m'lord.'

When they had gone, Richard poured Virginia and himself another glass.

'Well, well,' he said. 'Made an honest woman of her after all these years, and only because of what other people will think. What a funny people we are. Goodness, that would have made . . .'

He stopped. Virginia said, 'You were going to say "Marjorie laugh", weren't you?'

'Yes . . . I was.'

'I don't mind, darling. I've never minded. If they're as happy as you and I've been, they'll be very lucky.'

He went and kissed her tenderly and gratefully.

The servants' hall resounded as it had never done since the days of Sarah as Mr and Mrs Hudson's nuptials were celebrated that evening in whisky, gin, beer, stout and quantities of foodstuffs. Then, at one stage of the evening, Daisy managed to announce: 'Here, Mr Hudson! Eddie's got a surprise for you.'

They all looked at Edward, who protested that it was too late but was pushed by his wife through the door into the butler's pantry. He emerged some minutes later looking sheepish but smart in a brand new tailcoat.

Mr Hudson went to him. 'Edward! You mean to say . . . ?'

'I spoke to Lord Stockbridge about what you said, Mr Hudson, and he said, "Well, if that's Hudson's advice, we'll take it". So I'm to be butler, and there'll be another chap for the general duties.'

A general cheer went up and glasses were replenished.

'It suits you well, Edward,' Mr Hudson said. 'Mind that you always wear a high collar with it, though. None of those modern slipshod flat things.'

'I will, Mr Hudson.'

'That coat – your uniform – it is your badge of office. You are *the butler*. You are the one in charge of the house. A great responsibility will rest on your shoulders . . . a great deal of worry. If anything goes wrong, it is your fault, no one else's. If standards fall, it is your fault alone. You have tasted some of that responsibility already, Edward, but now you inherit the great tradition, centuries old, and I hope the training I have done my best to give you will always stand you in good stead.'

'Yes, Mr Hudson,' Edward said, a trifle huskily.

'Unhappily, there are not many households that can still afford proper servants. The world we have known seems to be falling about our ears. You are one of the lucky ones, my boy. One day you may be butler in a ducal household . . . a great honour and a great responsibility, so make sure you are always worthy of it. I would like to think that when you find yourself in any trouble or doubt, as you certainly must do from time to time, you will try to think what my action would have been in the circumstances, and that that will pull you through.'

Edward could only nod. Mrs Hudson was dabbing at her eyes.

Mr Hudson turned away to the sideboard, opened a drawer and drew out a book which Edward recognised at once. It had been temporarily in his care during Mr Hudson's illness.

'Here is a little gift for you. A legacy, you might almost call it.'

'Your . . . your pantry book . . . !'

'Take it, with my blessing – with the blessing of us all. I fancy you'll find a few wee wrinkles in it that the modern generation don't know much about.'

Edward took the book and returned his mentor's handshake, almost in tears. Daisy ran forward and kissed Mr Hudson on the cheek. Then Ruby, who had already drunk more than she could take, hiccuped, and everybody laughed, and the party went on again.

When the time had come for an end to be called, Edward and Daisy prepared to clear away the mess.

'No you don't,' Mrs Hudson said. 'Not on your last night here. Go on off to your flat.'

'I'll do it,' Rose volunteered.

'No you don't, neither. Off to bed you go, and leave Mr Hudson and me for a few minutes to ourselves.'

Edward and Daisy went. Rose gestured towards Ruby, fast asleep now, with her head on the table. Mrs Hudson waved her out. Her husband came to her side and together they looked down at the crumpled form, with the hair hanging untidily loose and the frock as creased as if she had been rolling on the floor in it.

'What are we going to do about her?' Mrs Hudson asked. 'We can't let her run loose on the streets like a stray dog. She could no more fend for herself in this town than an ostrich could.'

'I'm sure I don't know, Kate.' But he did. It was she who put it into words, though.

'We shall have to take her with us, Angus.'

He nodded.

'Why not? She can do some of the washing and the heavy work, the same as she does here.'

His wife looked at him censoriously. 'That wasn't my reason at all, Mr Hudson. My reason was Christian Charity.'

'Of course, my dear.'

He drew her to him and they kissed as decorously as befitted a newly-wed old butler and cook, about to become proprietor and proprietress of a respectable seaside establishment.

Ruby slept on as they cleared up around her. She was dreaming of John Barrymore. He was the Marquis of Something-or-other too foreign for her to pronounce. She had passed him on the stairs often and noticed how he had made a point of catching her eye.

And now, suddenly, there he was, coming down the steps into the servants' hall, his dress shirt gleaming in the half light, the diamond studs in it twinkling.

He strode across to her, wordlessly, and placed one arm around her waist. With the other hand he smoothed the hair from her brow. He leant forward, bending her backward, and his eager lips sought hers . . .

A clatter awoke her. Her dazed vision took in Mr Hudson

and Mrs B . . . – no, it was Mrs Hudson now – carrying glasses and bottles.

'What . . . what's happening?' she asked.

'Oh, nothing – 'cept we're doing your work for you,' Mrs Hudson replied. But she said it without any sarcasm; and Ruby wondered what she'd done for them both to be smiling at her so nice?